dəm

BOOKS BY WILLIAM MELVIN KELLEY

Dunsfords Travels Everywheres

dəm

A Drop of Patience

Dancers on the Shore

A Different Drummer

dəm

WILLIAM MELVIN KELLEY

FOREWORD BY JOHN S. WRIGHT

SK

Kelley

COFFEE HOUSE PRESS is an independent nonprofit literary publisher supported in part by a grant provided by the Minnesota State Arts Board, through an appropriation by the Minnesota State Legislature, and in part by a grant from the National Endowment for the Arts. Significant support has also been provided by Athwin Foundation; the Bush Foundation; Elmer L. & Eleanor J. Andersen Foundation; General Mills Foundation; Honeywell Foundation; the Givens Foundation for African American Literature; James R. Thorpe Foundation; Lila Wallace-Reader's Digest Fund; McKnight Foundation; The Medtronic Foundation; Pentair, Inc.; Patrick and Aimee Butler Family Foundation; The St. Paul Companies Foundation, Inc.; the law firm of Schwegman, Lundberg, Woessner & Kluth, P.A.; Star Tribune Foundation; the Target Foundation; West Group; and many individual donors. To you and our many readers across the country, we send our thanks for your continuing support.

COFFEE HOUSE PRESS books are available to the trade through our primary distributor, Consortium Book Sales & Distribution, 1045 Westgate Drive, Saint Paul, MN 55114. For personal orders, catalogs, or other information, write to: Coffee House Press, 27 North Fourth Street, Suite 400, Minneapolis, MN 55401.

LIBRARY OF CONGRESS CIP INFORMATION

Kelley, William Melvin, 1937-
   Dem / by William Melvin Kelly.
      p. cm.
   ISBN 1-56689-102-7 (alk. paper)
   1. Manhattan (New York, N.Y.)--Fiction. 2. Middle class men--Fiction. 3. WASPs (Persons)--Fiction. 4. Race relations--Fiction. 5. White men--Fiction. I. Title.
   PS3561.E392 D4 2001
   813'.54--DC21

                      00-065755

10 9 8 7 6 5 4 3 2 1

PRINTED IN CANADA

THIS BOOK IS DEDICATED TO
THE BLACK PEOPLE IN (NOT OF) AMERICA.

WMK

THE COFFEE HOUSE PRESS
BLACK ARTS MOVEMENT SERIES

The postwar 1920s was the decade of the "New Negro" and the Jazz Age "Harlem Renaissance," or first Black Renaissance of literary, visual, and performing arts. In the 1960s and 70s Vietnam War era, counterpointing the white backlash against the civil rights movement and rising Black Power insurgencies of SNCC, CORE, and the Black Panthers, a self-proclaimed "New Breed" generation of black artists and intellectuals orchestrated what they called the Black Arts Movement.

This energetic and highly self-conscious Black Arts Movement accompanied and helped foster an explosion of urban black popular culture analogous in many ways to the cultural renaissance of the earlier era: Broadway shows and off-Broadway independent black theater; African inspired painting and sculpture and postmodern graphics; music-minded performance poetry and streetcorner "rapping"; avant-garde "free jazz" with consciously cultivated Afro-Asian references and mystical spirituality; independent and Hollywood-based black cinema riveted on street life and the politics of the urban ghettos; politico-religious sects and charismatic orators like Malcolm X and Stokely Carmichael; "soul music" performers such as Ray Charles, James Brown, Aretha Franklin—and a host of writers—who celebrated and critiqued it all from the vantage point of a newly articulated Third World conscious "Black Aesthetic."

Although most of the literary commentary on the movement emphasizes Black Arts poetry and drama, African American novelists too walked the walk. The transformations of black consciousness produced corollary changes in the forms, styles, techniques, and ethos of all the African American literary modes. The Coffee House Press Black Arts Movement Series is devoted to reprinting unavailable works of the period. In selecting the titles, the editorial panel of African American authors and scholars has employed no fixed guidelines. We have looked for works with distinctive voices, with historical value as windows on the literary and social world of the time, and with that subjective and impressionistic quality of "aliveness" that crosses boundaries of audience, era, and topicality. We have tried to choose work that is masterful, that deserves another chance and other audiences, and that will help us keep the windows to the future open.

FOREWORD TO WILLIAM MELVIN KELLEY'S *dəm*
BY JOHN S. WRIGHT

In a 1967 interview published the same year his third novel, *dəm*, was released, William Melvin Kelley described himself as at a point in his career when he was becoming more experimental. At the same time he imagined himself retracing Faulkner's or Balzac's pattern of progressively "tying things together" in the overarching design of what, by the time he reached eighty, would hopefully coalesce into "one big book." That high ambition had nothing to do with wanting to write any of the vast new multiplotted tomes of avant-garde "maximal fiction" that would soon be identified with John Barth, William Gaddis, Thomas Pynchon, and Don DeLillo. Nor was Kelley looking backward to the old-fashioned panoramic trilogies and family sagas that had preoccupied scores of European and American realists from the middle of the nineteenth to the middle of the twentieth centuries. "To me," he asserted, "the greatest innovations of the novel are short, running from fifty to two hundred and fifty pages. Faulkner wrote naturally in a form which ran between fifty and seventy-five pages. Hemingway's novels were never too long. . . . If the writer turns out a seven-hundred-page novel, and works on it for a year, he can't have real control over the fiction; he can't pay the attention he should to prose rhythm, the close attention to the words that Hemingway or even Faulkner did." Big, sloppy novels "with lots of plots, lots of characters, but very little artistry" do not, he insisted, "make any revelations of the human being, the way he lives and thinks; they skim over life at a superficial level."

Kelley believed that it was the primary role of the artist "to educate men's hearts," more than their minds; that "our emotional education is far behind" what is necessary "to learn how to cope with our technological innovations"; and that such straits require true artists to "reveal things that human beings have never been exposed to in the novel before." His previous book, *A Drop of Patience* (1965), two hundred thirty-seven pages long, had taken him two years to write: "trying to get the prose right, the text, each nuance of thought and characterization and movement." That novel had grown out of his fascination with jazz musicians and his musings over the untimely death of Clifford Brown, the precocious jazz trumpeter who had blazed across the 1950s bebop firmament in the company of Art Blakey, Max Roach, and Sonny Rollins before a car accident stopped the flow of his virtuoso technique and original compositions. Kelley decided that it was time a black writer penned a really good novel about a jazz musician. Accordingly, "not for the sake of experiment, but for the sake of dimension," he decided to use only four senses to tell the tale—no visual imagery—and to bar the use of the verb "to hear," so that, in a novel devoted to the world of sound, he would not "clutter up the story" with endless repetitions of it. Because he had no interest in producing documentary fiction, he consciously kept his central character, Ludlow Washington, from being identifiable with any "real world" jazz counterpart, while nonetheless drawing on the living careers of "a great many great ones" for inspiration and pushing himself toward a novel that would instead create an alternate world of its own.

Kelley's personal heroes in fiction—John Hawkes, Nathanael West, Emily Brontë included—are all people who have managed to create their own world in fiction"; and he traced the genesis of *A Drop of Patience* to John Hawkes's influence on him as his first formal writing teacher. "Don't write about what you know; make it all up," Hawkes had counseled; and Kelley also heeded Hawkes's conviction that fiction created almost entirely out of the writer's imagination can be manipulated and controlled much better than the experientially derived.

Kelley's preoccupation with the elements of craft, with the meticulous making of architectonically and stylistically rationalized fiction, is not a commonly heralded signpost of that Black Power-driven 1960s insurgency variously called the Black Consciousness, or Black Aesthetic, or Black Arts Movement which was also claiming his attention and energies at the time. But Kelley's career was as closely allied with the emergence and mutations of the "New Breed" literary journals, writers' conferences, and creative outpourings as it was with the new, largely white cluster of avant-garde and experimental "metafictionists" and "black humorists." Along with Hawkes and John Barth and Pynchon and Joseph Heller, the new experimentalists were filling the literary void left by the 60s deaths of Hemingway, Faulkner, William Carlos Williams, e. e. cummings, and their older generation's modernist leadership. The evolving new configuration seemed increasingly to be a self-reflexive *post* modernism that Barth had dubbed "the Literature of Exhaustion" just two months before *dǝm* was released.

But the idea that fiction had reached a dead end, a point of exhausted possibilities, had little currency among the writers who had rallied to Larry Neal's and Amiri Baraka's call to forge black artists and black activists into one insuperable creative force. The New Breed black avant-garde envisioned, metaphorically at least, a literature not of exhaustion, but of high combustion—of "black fire"—as Baraka's and Neal's movement-mounting anthology proclaimed that year in its title. And they perceived themselves operating in a universe of linguistic possibilities expanding exponentially across the boundaries between the First World and the Third, the black world and the white, the old aesthetic canon and what free jazz partisans called "The New Thing." Kelley saw himself spiritually and aesthetically allied with the New Breed's new thing, and in an interview with Jervis Anderson insisted: "Our literary tradition is essentially the African literary tradition, which is not a written tradition. It is basically oral and I think black writers must begin to think in some of those terms, to use the fantastic oral language that has developed. . . . I find nothing in Ellison that I can use. I find nothing in Baldwin that I can use. LeRoi Jones and I are about the same age, and I feel that there are some similarities and some differences. But on the whole his sensibility is the one I'm closest to." Baraka's ethnomusicological theorizing and creative extrapolations in *Blues People* (1963) reinterpreted bop and modal jazz as a live spectrum of subversive models for reordering narrative space and time as well, for manipulating linguistic "color" and "texture" the way jazz modalists like Archie Shepp and Ornette Coleman and Cecil Taylor were miming aurally the visual experiments of Color Field and Action Painting. Like Baraka and the precocious figurative expressionist painter, Bob Thompson, whom Kelley met and whose cutting-edge use of flat patterns, "like silhouettes on rifle ranges" and "hallucinating visions with the content of fairy stories" he came to see as a visualization of his own linguistic cosmology, Kelly committed himself to formulating a contra-canonical aesthetics and "some type of philosophy that will help us get free."

A native New Yorker and son of the editor of the Harlem-based black newspaper, *The Amsterdam News*, Kelley had first begun distinguishing himself as a writer by winning literary prizes while still an undergraduate at Harvard. Then, after jettisoning degree plans for a life-changing full devotion to fiction, he won fellowships from the John Hay Whitney Foundation and the National Institute of Arts and Letters, which enabled him to finish his first novel, *A Different Drummer*, in 1962. The Black Arts Movement's primary literary organ, *Negro Digest* (renamed *Black World* in 1970) showcased Kelley as part of the "New Wave" of cross-media black talent (along with actor James Earl Jones and dancer Alvin Ailey) as early as October 1962. Reviews of his subsequent work, by Black Arts poetry doyen Dudley Randall, for example, appeared routinely in its pages, along with Kelley's own essays and short fiction, during the following years.

Apparently begun during a class with Hawkes at Harvard, *A Different Drummer* won mixed praise from reviewers on both sides of the color line, who routinely compared it with James Baldwin's *Another Country* or John A. Williams's *Sissie* or John Killens's *'Sippi* (all also published that year) and occasionally with releases by white writers as diverse as Doris Lessing, Philip Roth, Faulkner, and Isaac Bashevis Singer. Most of the commentary noted Kelley's distinctive voice, his technical dexterity, and the book's mythic resonances. But most were also troubled by *A Different Drummer*'s violations of realist conventions, or its disconcerting mixture of history with fantasy, or its want of "constructive" application to current racial conflicts. On the book jacket, Archibald MacLeish, another of Kelley's writing mentors at Harvard, acknowledged praisefully that "American Negroes have been mythmakers in tales and tunes from the beginning of their culture, but here is a young Negro novelist who has used that mysterious power in a new way: he has imagined, not a myth of time gone, but a myth of time going—a myth for now." To the *Kenyon Review*'s white commentator, however, Kelley's work was novelistic double trouble. Damnably, it was a book about the South by a man who had never lived there. Moreover, it was allegedly symptomatic of an invading fleet of new fictions that were no longer fuelling themselves on "dependable old Story" but instead on some Nuclear Age Fuel X "refined from the crude energies of Freud's enormous head, a pool under the desert—with a few lumps of Story thrown into it." Across the color line, *Phylon*'s black reviewer opened his survey of significant belles lettres by and about Negroes published in 1962" with a paean of praise for Baldwin's *Another Country*, and then found newcomer Kelley's volume "in some ways a better book." But the virtues he ascribed to *A Different Drummer* were those dear to the increasingly moribund traditions of bourgeois racial uplift: "the major characters are more respectable and wholesome"; "the experiences of the characters and the language by which they communicate their experiences are more acceptable to readers of normal sensibilities"; and "the racial overtones which are basic to both books are more subdued and indirectly expressed."

What most of these reviewers shared, regardless of racial affiliation, was a critical imagination bound to the conventions of inbred realist verisimilitude—"rounded" three-dimensional characters, "psychologically credible" motivation, causally coherent plots, recognizable locales, concepts of human dignity and nobility derived from Christian humanism, and a decorous racial etiquette (that was overtaxed at the time by the decidedly indecorous racial warfare of the era). Interpreters such as these were ill-equipped to respond to the decidedly antirealist fictive premises upon which Kelley's novel was structured, or to the radical "neo-black" consciousness with which it was infused. Kelley had taken Hawkes's road to imaginative autonomy, and the New Breed's freedom train to cultural consciousness. It wasn't necessary to have been born and raised in the South to know it well enough to write about it, he announced inside the book jacket: "A Negro knows the South by osmosis. Every Negro seems to have a grandparent or other relative who packed up and followed Hope northward. The South is the Negro's Old Country." Kelley's fictional world would be no more bound to the documentary history of that Old Country than was Faulkner's mythopoetic Yoknapatawpha.

In fact parodying Faulkner's devices of fictive documentation from *Go Down, Moses*, Kelley opened *A Different Drummer* with "an excerpt from *The Thumbnail Almanac*, 1961 . . . page 643" describing an imaginary Southern state, admitted to the Union back in 1818, which was the home of Confederate General Dewey Willson, whose descendants had controlled the government and the economy for generations, right up to the notated "Recent History" which highlights the mysterious departure in June 1957 "of all the state's Negro inhabitants." According to an official declaration by the current white governor, "we never needed them, never wanted them, and we'll get along fine without them." But Kelley's debut novel proceeds to fashion an array of opposing, intersubjective truths and apperceptions, through the deft use of multiple point of view and stream of consciousness narration, fabricated journal entries, and storefront palaver—all from the perspective of the white inhabitants of the imaginary town of Sutton, who can sense but never really comprehend what has brought the black exodus about. The central character and active agent in all that has transpired here is a legendary African slave's modern-day descendant, Tucker Caliban, who one day stuns the town by purchasing and then ritually destroying the ancestral land, property, and all other symbolic vestiges of his family's enslavement. Tucker's desecrations cum purifications are a mystery resolvable to the white Suttonians and Kelley's readers alike only in the fragments of history and motive divulged sparingly and in chronological disarray throughout the remaining pages. Readers are forced to confront and decipher the processes of history and mythopoesis as revealed by a narrative that incorporates enigmatically the power and mutability of European and African oral tradition, the ideals and dystopic legacy of nineteenth-century Transcendentalism, and an apocalyptic biblical prophecy—all filtered through an antirealist method that blends elements of fantasy, allegory, naturalism, and the French nouveau roman, or antinovel.

With the customary lag between creative practice and critical comprehension, half a decade later Robert Scholes provided readers and reviewers alike a language and set of concepts for grappling with novels such as this in a critical study called *The Fabulators*, published the same year *dəm* appeared, in 1967. Scholes used the term *fabulation* to describe a mode of fiction that presents a world radically discontinuous from yet cognitively related to our own, a form of postrealistic creation energized by self-conscious attention to design, a "delight in formal and verbal dexterity," and a didactic or satirical intent. Such work was actually descended from Henry James's explorations in the inherent unreliability of words—and the consequent unreliability of narrators—and it was closely allied with the 1960s Black Humor literary movement with which, Scholes thought, "most of this country's exciting young writers are connected in some way." He cited Albee, Barth, Donleavy, Friedman, Hawkes, Heller, Purdy, Pynchon, Southern, and Vonnegut (no writers of color or women caught his eye).

In the hands of these new fabulators the sensibility and compassion which characterized the great novels of the nineteenth century were being modified by the postmodern wit and "cruelty" of Black Humor. Horace Walpole's eighteenth-century epigram about life being tragic for those who feel and comic for those who think was another premodern antecedent. But the impress of the Nuclear Age on the old traditions of satire and picaresque that Walpole knew had mushroomed in the atomic era into something beyond traditional satire. There were two kinds of fabulation, Scholes suggested: one, the "dogmatic," operates out of a closed system and functions like a modern analogue to religious romances; the other, the "speculative," arises from the remnants of humanistic tradition and incorporates facets of the Scientific Romance associated with the novels of H.G. Wells—its dystopian strain in particular. The satirical edge on most dystopian and anti-utopian writing had become jagged and unremediating in the new fabulations, so that fabulative satire was "less certain ethically but more certain esthetically than traditional satire." Reflecting quite properly their heritage from the esthetic movement of the nineteenth century and the ethical relativism of the twentieth, the fabulators "have some faith in art but they reject all ethical absolutes. Especially, they reject the traditional satirist's faith in the efficacy of satire as a reforming instrument." Most tellingly, they are inclined to put their faith in the humanizing value of dark laughter; and whatever changes they hope to work in their readers are "the admittedly evanescent changes inspired by art, which need to be continually renewed, rather than the dramatic renunciations of vice and folly postulated by traditional satire."

Of all the fabulators, Hawkes most closely approximated the conviction of the leading French antinovelist, Alain Robbe-Grillet, that the raw phenomenon of human experience—not abstracted, not internalized, not anthropomorphized by metaphor—is the proper subject matter for writers trying to represent reality without imposed interpretations. Like the antinovelists, Hawkes's manner as a fabulator seemed predicated on the techniques of Freudian or Lacanian psychoanalysis, and the process of forcing the conscious mind to expose and liberate the sources of its anxiety by reconstructing "reality" from the disordered fragments of unmediated waking and fantasy experience. In 1965, the year Kelley released *A Drop of Patience*, the novel attributed directly to teacherly influence, Hawkes made his stance clear in an interview:

> My novels are not highly plotted, but certainly they're elabo-
> rately structured. I began to write fiction on the assumption that
> the true enemies of the novel were plot, character, setting, and
> theme, and having once abandoned these familiar ways of
> thinking about fiction, totality of vision or structure was really
> all that remained. And structure—verbal and psychological
> coherence—is still my largest concern as a writer. Related or cor-
> responding event, recurring image and recurring action, these
> constitute the essential substance or meaningful density of my
> writing. . . . The success of the effort depends on the degree and
> quality of consciousness that can be brought to bear on fully
> liberated materials of the unconscious. I'm trying to hold in
> balance poetic and novelistic methods in order to make the
> novel a more valid and pleasurable experience.

To Hawkes, the pleasures of the novel—of reading it and of creating it—refer, Scholes recognized, not to the pleasures of wish-fulfillment, as in simple romance, nor to the joy of perceiving a world ordered and rationalized by comic vision, as in intellectual comedy or satire, but instead to the psychic release of confronting our fears and fantasies in order to wrestle with them, rather than flee from them.

Kelley's allegiances to Hawkes's theory of fiction and to the methods of fabulation seem manifest in many ways; but Kelley's original-ity as an artist lies more precisely in the ways he has placed these allegiances in service to an African American cultural cosmology and its imperatives. *A Different Drummer* was indeed a new kind of *fabulative* black satire, steeped in the processes and mysterious powers of orality and determined to foreground postmodern apprehensions about the inherent arbitrariness of words. *A Different Drummer* underscored the *fableness* of the political and social world and postulated characters whose true nature we can never plumb, worlds we can never penetrate. Yet this first novel was not so much a break with, as a rechanneling of, patterns quite familiar to black readers, writers, and raconteurs. The legend of the giant African slave had been a staple of antebellum folk legend and slave narrative; and the book's central motif of a wholesale disappearance of the black population had earlier been worked to great effect in George Schuyler's 1931 satiric near future fantasy, *Black No More: Being an Account of the Strange and Wonderful Workings of Science in the Land of the Free, A.D. 1933-1940*. In Schuyler's fable the black exodus is effected through the "electro-glandular nutrition control" invention of a black scientific genius who enables his brethren to denigrify and then "migrate," not northward, as Tucker Caliban does in Kelley's tale, but across the ocular color line, where they disappear into the white race. In 1960, two years before *A Different Drummer* was published, the same speculative motif of a suddenly vanishing black populace resurfaced in preliminary plans to produce a one-act play by Douglas Turner Ward called *Day of Absence: A Satirical Fantasy*, which was finally staged in New York in 1965.

Ward, who would soon become the founder of the Negro Ensemble Company and one of the leading figures in the Black Arts theater movement, had created a satire on Southern racism which he described as "a reverse minstrel show done in white face": Fourteen black actors in white makeup and blonde wigs turn the century-old blackface tradition on its head and bring to life the comic conceit of a small town of Southern whites awakening one sultry morning to discover themselves completely abandoned by their black maids, butlers, mammies, factory and farm workers—and facing immediate social and economic crisis. Part medieval morality play, part expressionistic situational burlesque, this reverse minstrel show had a dual genesis. Ward had been a Southern-born political activist and transplanted Northern journalist earlier in his career and had first conceived the idea for *Day of Absence* in the wake of the 1955 Montgomery, Alabama bus boycott and the manifestly absurd images of white drivers daily recirculating empty buses along empty routes in search of disappeared black passengers. But the dramaturgy for translating this bizarre public ritual into theatrical terms was finally sparked by his 1961 experience in the cast of the landmark three-year-long, 1,408 performance run of Frenchman Jean Genet's *Les Negres*, or *The Blacks*, at the off-Broadway St. Mark's Playhouse in New York.

Produced first in Paris in 1959, then translated to the London and New York stages in 1961, *The Blacks* made theater history as off-Broadway's longest running nonmusical play ever mounted. It galvanized largely white audiences in America from the day of its opening, May 4, 1961, when it shared newspaper headlines with CORE and SNCC's first Freedom Ride confrontations with the segregated South. *The Blacks* played on through a second year of staging against the backdrop of nationwide urban race riots, and a third year accompanied by over 10,000 organized racial protests coast to coast, together with a split in the civil rights movement that presaged the rise of Black Power, the Black Panthers, and an apotheosized Malcolm X. *The Blacks* arrived in America with its author already mythologized by Jean Cocteau and Jean Paul Sartre as the avant-garde's own archetypal outsider—a precocious bastard, thief, beggar, male prostitute, pornographer, and convict who had transmogrified himself into contemporary France's greatest and most disquieting writer. Genet was being bracketed along with Samuel Beckett and Eugene Ionesco as one of the major innovators in the absurdist and neo-surrealist transformation of Western drama; and within a few years he would be stumping for the Panthers and the P.L.O. *The Blacks* was his calculated dual assault on the conventions of naturalistic theater and the politics of racial domination. The play proceeds by abandoning the logic of plot and character for cultivated artificiality, for shifting levels and fragmented forms of reality and illusion, and for human action reduced to caricature by ensembles of mime, masks, and mirrors. Dramaturgically at the opposite end of the spectrum from political agitprop, *The Blacks* was a multimedia exercise in "total theatre"—music, dance, rhythm, and ritual—that was structured on at least three levels. On the first, a group of seemingly ordinary blacks—a cook, sewing maid, student, prostitute, and so forth—come together to enact an entertainment, a "clown show," centered on the symbolic murder and entombment of a white woman by a black rebel, together with the trial of the murderer, all of which is witnessed, on the second level, by part of the group who are up in a gallery and masked grotesquely as whites, until from outside this play within a play, at the third level, a "real" black political rebel enters and reveals the actions in the theater to be merely a white-designed diversion from the "real world" action offstage—the execution of a "real" black traitor for betraying a secret society of black conspirators against "real world" white rule.

Genet made it explicit in his preface that *The Blacks* is a play "written . . . by a white man . . . [and] intended for a white audience," though it originated in a dialectically opposing pretext: "One evening an actor asked me to write a play for an all-black cast." Genet had quickly perceived, however, that this seemingly simple charge entailed a pair of interlocking conundrums: "But what exactly is a black? First of all, what's his color?" Genet's dramaturgical answers gave the completed play an ontological and perspectival twist. On its first level, *The Blacks* focuses less on black reality than on the stereotypes and fantasies imposed on black people by the white world. The roles played by the unmasked black actors are hyperbolic caricatures of the black images nurtured by the white spectators for whom the play is intended. Ingrained brutality, cannibal proclivities, odiferous bodies, and rapacious sexuality are compounded in a projective fantasy that leads to the seduction and "murder" of the white woman, whose crucial role in the ritual is reenacted by a black male in symbolic drag: "a blond wig, a crude cardboard carnival mask representing a laughing white woman with big cheeks, a piece of knitting, two balls of wool, a knitting needle, and white gloves." The masked blacks, representing the white judges, portray what their unmasked comrades imagine is the white perception of black reality, so that in the trial of the black "murderer" before these "whites," the account of his homicidal hatred *gratifies* his judges. During the reenactment, the white woman's domineering, hypochondriacal mother and cuckolded husband are mimed in absentia by the blacks, the clownishness of their display counterbalancing the cultivated horror of the scene, in her own home, where the miscegenous coupling and the killing ultimately take place. After the intrusion of the "real world" trial, the black actors return to the play within a play, ultimately execute the court of white-masked superiors and, as the curtain falls, turn their backs on the presumably white audience.

In the inevitable furor the play aroused, writers on both sides of the American color line found themselves divided on its merits and implications. Since the violence of *The Blacks* was purely verbal, and channeled by indirection away from the intended white audience, it enabled the *New York Times* reviewer, for instance, to describe the play as a "lyrical tone poem for the theater" which provides a voyeuristic "exploration into the heart of the Negro." Violence of this sort disturbed white critics less than the "nihilistic values [it] propounds in opposition to the positive values of Western bourgeois Graeco-Christian society, values such as work, family, country, love, respect for life and property, the high values of art and culture." Because *The Blacks* came from a famous white French author and an avant-garde tradition they heeded, white spectators often found the play less offensive than did black Americans, who reacted more to its dispiriting message about the ultimate futility of revolt and its visceral embrace of loathsome black images than to its metatheatrical form.

As already noted, however, Ward found Genet's work powerfully influential for his own creative development and maintained that the Frenchman wrote more honestly and freely about blacks and the white world than many African American writers who devoted themselves to countering racial stereotypes and presenting "positive images." Less laudatory than Ward, Jones, whose own fiction and plays during the era incorporated many concepts and techniques from absurdist and surrealist European precursors, worked out dramaturgically his own dialectical critique of Genet's premises in a play called *The Great Goodness of Life: A Coon Show*, which also premiered in *dɘm*'s reverberant year of release, 1967. Jones's "coon show" was an explicit response to Genet's "clown show." It extracts and then inverts several of Genet's dramatic situations (the theatrical game of the play within a play, the ritual murder, the trial). It supplants the intended white audience for a black one, purges a "royal court" of petit bourgeois blacks instead of whites, and utterly rejects the controlling metaphor that, as an absurdist principle, makes black identity merely a figurative mirror of whiteness.

Drawing us closer yet to the contextual world of Kelley's *dɘm*, two other African American literary figures of the time, playwright Lorraine Hansberry and novelist John Killens, provide other crucial glimpses of the ripple effect *The Blacks* generated in African American literary circles. Hansberry's reaction was chronicled by *The Village Voice* in a volatile exchange with irascible novelist-cum-pugilist Norman Mailer during the weeks following *The Blacks*' 1961 New York premiere.

Mailer had written a frenzied two-part review of the play (incorporated in 1964 into an essayistic stew called *The Presidential Papers*) in which he deemed it "a hot hothouse tense livid off-fag deep-purple voodoo Mon Doo production, thick, jungle bush, not unjazzy, never cool, but at its worst . . . the truest and most explosive play anyone has yet written at all about the turn in the tide, and the guilt and horror in the white man's heart as he turns to face his judge." The horror worked in the *black* man's heart, on Genet's stage, and in the real world since the Second War, Mailer proclaimed, was the same disease of ethnic assimilation into middle-class America that afflicted the Jews—"the mass communication of nothingness into their personality" by the same "slavery of ascent" that the Geist of Liberal Totalitarianism "imposes on all of us." Among the black bourgeoisie, the longing after whiteness that Genet dissected in *The Blacks* produced "a parody of the white bourgeoisie" that, as Mailer saw it, kept the black bourgeoisie from knowing that they are part of "a militant people moving toward inevitable and much-deserved victory: They cannot know because they have not seen themselves from outside (as we have seen them), that there is a genius in their race—it is possible that Africa is closer to the root of whatever life is left than any other land."

In her retort Lorraine Hansberry lumped Mailer and Genet together as the architects of an avant-garde "New Paternalism" steeped in romantic racism and the desperate certainty that "if the self-appointed 'top' of society is as utterly rotten as it is, then the better side of madness must be the company and deistic celebration of 'the bottom.' " Despite Genet's inventive poetry and exquisite theatrical mind, *The Blacks*, she noted, was "more than anything else a conversation between white men about *themselves*" in which the blacks remain exotic shadows, and guilt-ridden white audiences retain their distance and their sense of difference from the lives represented, masked or unmasked, on stage. Mailer's self-defining "White Negro" hipster mythology notwithstanding, she insisted, "how can Mailer or Genet . . . really be expected to know, really know, that the commonplace *reverse* assumptions among Negroes about everybody else ('The Others') are just as touching, innocent, and vicious?. . . Is it not 'known' among Negroes that white people, as an entity, are 'dirty' (especially white women who never seem to do their own cleaning);

inherently cruel (the cold fierce roots of Europe: who else would put all those people into ovens scientifically); 'smart' ('you really have to hand it to the m.f.'s')," etc. Among the oppressed the mystique of otherness could be combined with a sense of moral superiority as tenaciously as their opposites were among the whites, Hansberry observed; but these were not mirror reflections, and they were not "sealed in the loins by genetic mysteries."

Mailer believed unabashedly then "that there were qualities, essences, innate differences of being between black and white"; and he maintained that at the root of racism in the liberal mind lay the Western fear of the body—its existential demands and orgasmic moments of animal unreason. He insisted that "what is at stake in the twentieth century is not the economic security of man—every bureaucrat in the world lusts to give us this—it is, on the contrary, the peril that they will extinguish the animal in us." But to Hansberry, economic and political forces defined the world's preeminent problem: "the oppression of man by man; it is this which threatens existence. And it is this which Genet evades with an abstraction." Since early 1960 she had been at work on the first major drama by an African American playwright to focus on the black African struggle for liberation, a stubbornly naturalistic play set against the historical backdrop of the early 1950s Mau Mau revolt against British colonial rule in Kenya. In the wake of *The Blacks*, she reconceived her own script in order "to confront Guilt with a greater imperative: the necessity for action—that is, to *do* something about it." Half in jest, she prefaced it with Genet's opening query, "But what exactly is a black? First of all, what's his color?"—and titled her work-in-progress *Les Blancs*, as an ironic inversion.

John Oliver Killens and Hansberry were close colleagues, both active in the Harlem Writers Guild; and in the essays collected in his own inversionary *Black Man's Burden* (1965), Killens carried Hansberry's sortie one step further. "Who will tell the real story of America if the black writer doesn't?" he asked:

> Certainly not the gentlemen of the "mainstream" who still believe in Gunga Din and Uncle Tom and Aunt Jemima, *or* the "avant-garde," the rebels who are really anti-revolutionary. Jean

Genet and his genre, the "theater of the absurd," the "beatnik," the "new wave" . . . Few white American writers care enough about the country to criticize it fundamentally. Compared with the ambivalent lot who clutter up the mainstream, they make up a pitifully small pool of courageous talent. . . . One hopes that one day at least one of them will care deeply enough to dramatize or novelize the white folk who are completely taken in by the "righteous" cause of white supremacy, explain them to us and particularly to themselves in all their myriad contradictions. What is the metamorphosis of a racial bigot? Are they born retarded? Is it fed to them with their mother's milk? The public schools? The press? The church? The mass-communications media? How? Why? When? Where? America needs to understand what goes into the making of a man who will go out on a Sunday morning in Birmingham, Alabama, and participate in the strange ritual of throwing bombs into a church and killing innocent little Negro children. . . . And what about the sickness of men who will stand on the sidelines and watch such bloody rituals enacted, without daring to speak? What sort of unspeakable fear has locked their jaws? What is the true anatomy of racial prejudice? Here is a challenge for some writer who cares.

Killens had published his title essay as the closing piece in *Ebony* magazine's August, 1965 special issue, *The White Problem in America*, in which the rhetoric of inversion was comprehensively deployed, and a gallery of black artists and activists (including Baldwin, organizer Whitney Young, journalists Carl Rowan and Louis Lomax, psychiatrist Kenneth Clark, and theologian Martin Luther King, Jr.) collectively took up historian Lerone Bennett's proposition that "there is no Negro problem in America. The problem of race in America, insofar as that problem is related to packets of melanin in men's skins, is a white problem. And in order to solve that problem we must seek its source, not in the Negro but in the white American. . . . When we say that the causes of the race problem are rooted in the white American and the white community, we mean that the power is the white American's and so is the responsibility. We mean that the white American created, *invented* the race problem and that his fears and frailties are responsible for the urgency of the problem ... that because he is a problem to himself he has made others problems to themselves." The corresponding analyses of white hate groups, white guilt, the white liberal, the typical white suburbanite, white sexual fears of blacks, and the white power structure ranged from the scientific to the polemical to the speculative—interspersed strategically with doses of cartoon humor and cathartic jokes, but all devoted to the psychosocial project of inversion, redefinition, reorientation.

Begun by Kelley during the aftermath of the Genet firestorm and fully abreast of this reorienting black consciousness, *dəm* represents one African American novelist's expressive and decidedly experimental effort to create a fictional work of lasting value out of the era's complex political and perspectival struggle over the nature of American social reality. In the 1964 preface to his collection of short stories, *Dancers on the Shore*, Kelley had been explicit, however, about his own literary discomfort with the imperatives of problem solving. "An American writer who happens to have brown skin faces this unique problem," he wrote: "Solutions and answers to The Negro Problem are very often read into his work.... At this time, let me say for the record that I am not a sociologist or a politician or a spokesman. Such people try to give answers. A writer, I think, should ask questions. He should depict people, not symbols or ideas disguised as people." And what all people hold in common, he had concluded in an earlier essay, is that "it is in the nature of man ... to search constantly for an absolute truth in which he can believe, be it God, Jesus, the Blessed Virgin, Allah, Art, Country, Home, Mother, or Race. It does not seem to matter that his search turns up chaos under apparent order; man searches for his absolute anyway." In *dəm*, the search for absolutes and the revelation of chaos beneath apparent order give this novel a mythopoetic resonance even as the concrete devices of fabulation and the dialectics of bitter, blue-black satire undermine the mythologies upon which the disintegrating lives of the white central characters depend.

After two novels and a collection of short stories all revolving around black protagonists and the interconnected but subordinate lives of white contemporaries, *dəm*'s primary focus on the Manhattan world of a WASP ad man struck critics like those of the *Saturday Review* as "a jarring surprise." Kelley's protagonist, Mitchell Pierce, the reviewer objected, "is upper-middle-class white, an advertising copywriter, emotionally and sexually impotent, a travesty of a man. His wife, Tam, is a domineering bitch whose principal characteristics are her penchant for ridicule and her preoccupation with her hairdo. Tam's mother is the third leading figure; she too is cold, manipulative, discreetly savage." Able to recognize the fictional world of these characters cognitively as a grotesque "nightmare vision," the critic nevertheless insisted emotionally that the writer treat their actions and motives with "subtlety," "sympathy," and "understanding" —and in so doing voiced an ambivalence common to many white readers. With a different twist, so did the reviewer for the *Prairie Schooner*, who interpreted the book's title and its dedication ("to The Black people in [not of] America") as signals to read the book as "a realistic report of the relationships of the races in contemporary America." Accordingly, "for a time, when Mitchell Pierce wanders through Harlem in search of the black man who has fathered one of his wife's twins, William Melvin Kelley's *dəm* seems almost real. The texture of the language, the settings, and the dialogue, give the reader a sense of life, of the alienation of a confused white man who suspects he is on the periphery of a life-rhythm more natural and substantial than his own." But this particular reader felt himself betrayed when the novel offered him no comforting way out of its world of self-deluded, self-destructive "pasteboard, bloodless whites." That an experience of confusion and confrontation might be precisely what the novelist had intended, the *Schooner* critic interpreted not as device of artistic revelation but as revenge—of which he and other white readers were presumably the primary object.

Kelley's own rationale, however, proposes a quite different angle of vision on *dəm*. "I've written it for black people," he told Jervis Anderson in the interview for *Dissent*. "I've turned the whole process on its head. Instead of writing about what American society has done to black people, I've tried to write about American society in terms of what it is doing to itself and what it is. If black people read it, they can understand what America is and why it is doing what it is doing to them." In other words, revelation is *dəm*'s primary purpose, not revenge; but black readers, not white ones, are its primary intended audience. And beyond its title and dedication, its other opening "signals"—a pair of epigraphs, a scientific note, and a typographically puzzling narrative lead—prepare its presumptively black readers for a fabricated world beyond that of realistic report.

The first epigraph, literate and canonically American, comes in fact from F. Scott Fitzgerald's *The Great Gatsby*: "His dream must have seemed so close that he could hardly fail to grasp it. He did not know that it was already behind him, somewhere in that vast obscurity beyond the city, where the dark fields of the republic rolled on under the night." It evokes the self-deceptive, delusional power of an archetypal American hero's American Dream, the entanglement of his romantic personal quest with political hegemony, and his unheroic condition of dreamily disordered consciousness. The second epigraph, oral and extra-canonically African, is an Ashanti proverb about the decay of empire: "The ruin of a nation begins in the homes of its people." Together the epigraphs create a dialectic that the novel ahead unfolds in a fictional world that is somehow affected, the next page notifies us, by an esoteric phenomenon of reproductive biology called "superfecundation." This we learn, with the authorizing voice of science to soothe our incredulity, makes it possible for a woman to bear fraternal twins who are not the customary outcome of different fertilizing sperm from a single male, but who instead are born of sperm from separate couplings with two different males. Finally, on the last page before the narrative proper begins, we are greeted with a vernacular storyteller's opening "hook"—"now lemme tell you how dem folks live." But rather than being rendered in the familiar roman alphabetical characters conventionally used to represent the sound and structure of "nonstandard" spoken dialects, it is instead transcribed in the International Phonetic Association system of modified Roman, Latin, and Greek characters; of reversed letters and fused diagraph symbols: scientific markers for self-contained linguistic systems of coded sounds and meanings.

Kelley prepares us to discover a context for his book's title, and for the novel as a whole, in the signals that lead to this hieroglyphic hook line: a storytelling world with its own language, laws of behavior, teleology, and ideal audience. This particular hook is a raconteur's well-worn point of entry to that world of wry vernacular "lies," tall tales, and calculated distortion which deploys outrageous exaggeration and hyperbolic imagery within the framework of an ostensibly realistic story—in order to involve, entertain, and instruct an audience. In the vernacular world, tall tales (whose purposes are customarily fictional and comic) consciously blur their borders with myth and legend (which are customarily vehicles for serious belief) by using the devices of realism to "set up" the listener for action on superhuman or supernatural levels. American hero-worship has depended heavily on a confusion between the heroes of frontier myth or history and the heroes of tall tales; and Mark Twain, for one, mastered the literary technique of manipulating the narrative frame by using "realistic" and "reliable" bourgeois narrators to set his audiences up for the hyperbolic yarns of tall tale heroes—yarns told with a wink in the teller's eye. Kelley believed that, in the evolution of the American novel away from its European predecessors, Twain had found the key to "breaking the novel open" for new ideas in such uses of vernacular narrative. So in *dəm*, where Kelley's own objective is to break the novel form open even further—for the infusion of African American experience and ideas—he inverts Twain's stratagem and deploys an authorizing black vernacular voice to "set up" a hyperbolic fable of white bourgeois experience.

Accordingly, the difference between reading *dəm* as "a realistic report of the relationships of the races in contemporary America" rather than as "one of the outstanding comic novels of the last decade," which the reviewer for the *Boston Globe* aptly did, may depend on something as elementary or as astute as being able to distinguish a wink from a blink in the imagined eye of the novelist. But even critics with such insight were forced to acknowledge that, on its face, the book is also "a frightening story of white Americans utterly controlled and deluded by fantasies—and Negroes quietly watching, laughing, and hating." On the 1969 paperback edition of *dəm*, which was subtitled "a black man's slashing satire of life in white America," a split-view cartoonish cover illustration presents the left side image of a child-sized, open-mouthed, marionette-faced adult white male, wearing a striped business suit and carrying an attaché case. He is seated, with one shoe off and one shoe on, in an infant's high chair and being spoon fed by a solicitous black housemaid. On the illustration's right side, but recessed, a full-sized white female marionette sits at a mirror in a dressing gown and hair net, her legs long and languorously crossed, before a table of perfumes and beauty potions.

In his introduction to this first paperback edition, Ghanaian philosopher Willie Abraham described the book's spotlight on figures like these as *almost* placing it within the tradition of the so-called "raceless" black novel in America. The reference here is to a line of serious fictions about white life written by black authors—from Paul Laurence Dunbar at the turn of the century to Frank Yerby, Willard Motley, Chester Himes, and Ann Petry during the first post-wwii decade—who were either weary of literary ghettoization, eager to demonstrate their cosmopolitanism, or riding periodic crests of integrationist optimism. But Kelley's satiric subversion of conventional seriousness, coupled with his New Breed black consciousness, leave the sober tradition of "raceless" integrationism far behind. Houston Baker, who considered *dəm* to be primarily a racially nonpartisan send-up of "twentieth-century, bureaucratic, impotent man," perceived its white main characters as archetypes "vibrant in the underconsciousness of Black America," part of the legions of "Sir Charles, the white knight" who serve as foils, and as privileged prey, for the hustler kingpins of a new black literary cityscape.

But as cartoon characters, society marionettes, and Main Street inhabitants of mainstream consciousness, the forebears of Mitchell Pierce, his wife Tam, and his mother-in-law had emerged as highly defined stock characters in the urban mythology of mid-twentieth-century American literary comedy decades before Kelley conceived his satiric inversion of American race matters. Instructively for Kelley, Langston Hughes, as early as the fourteen stories of *The Ways of White Folks* (1934), had lambasted white hypocrisy and liberal paternalism in its myriad personas, using a scathing style reminiscent of H. L. Mencken to unmask the self-deception, mendacity, sham, and sanctimoniousness of middlebrow white Negrophiles and Negrophobes. And five short years before *dəm*, Chester Himes, in a Rabelaisian "experiment in goodwill" called *Pinktoes* (1961), had cast a bemused eye and a punning tongue on the ethical lapses, social pretensions, and sexual excesses of caricaturish white liberals and their "striver's row" peers among the black bourgeoisie, who together dedicate themselves, body more than soul, to solving "The Negro Problem" through the doublespeak foreplay of "interracial intercourse." But neither Hughes nor Himes put to focused use the specifically archetypal leverage that Sinclair Lewis, James Thurber, Robert Benchley, S. J. Perelman, and West had provided through extensive elaboration, between the 1920s and the 1950s, of a modern and distinctly white American comic antihero far more pervasive and less disconcerting than Mailer's countercultural White Negro.

Walter Blair and the historians of American popular culture generally concur that, in the transition from the nineteenth to the twentieth century, American humor registered the changes in society more explicitly than any other form of writing. A tradition whose humorists were almost all rustic or western until the 1920s had changed radically thereafter, through urbanization and industrialization. The old corpus of rascally but strong and competent Yankee or "cracker-barrel" frontier heroes was swiftly replaced in metropolitan magazines like the *New Yorker* by a pitiable specimen of comic incompetency and "perfect neuroticism," as Benchley termed it: a frustrated, fugitive, slightly eccentric Little Man besieged by his own ineptitude and by his unending encounters with overwhelming women, bosses, bureaucracies, and technology. Sexually repressed, socially inept, and thoroughly dominated by Amazonian wives, mothers-in-law, and intractable servants, these middle-class Little Men with middle-class angles of vision lead lives engulfed in domestic trivia and the depradations of massive workplace and government organizations. Beset by neurotic fears, childlike insecurity, and recurring threats to their sanity, the Little Men have neither the capacity nor the will for political engagement and are forced underground, so to speak, to the inner world of daydream and fantasy where, like Thurber's Walter Mitty, they fight back in small, secret ways—and occasionally eke out a small inner victory in the face of pervasive outer defeat.

Minnesota-born Sinclair Lewis had given archetypal significance to a not fully urbanized precursor of the type in *Babbitt* (1922), with its satirical portrait of a middle-class Middlewestern yes-man bred on intolerance and complacent conformity, a vacuous shell of a man who "hustles for hustle's sake" to sell consumer salesmanship to droves of Babbitt wannabes, while leading a life of quintessential mediocrity and family dysfunction devoted to "mechanical business, mechanical religion, mechanical golf and dinner parties, and mechanical conversation with mechanical friends." At the very end of his literary career, Lewis transported a variation of his archetype of white middlebrow mediocrity across the color line in *Kingsblood Royal* (1947), through the fictive genealogical discovery of a racially tainted family tree, which punctures the title character's smug assurance of his own white, Protestant, Aryan superiority and sends him careening through the Du Boisian Veil of Color into a bruisingly grotesque netherworld experience as a passing-light "Negro." Unlike the *New Yorker* cohort, Lewis, however, worked out of a framework closer to venerable Menippean satire, with linear narrative structure and tightly controlled intellectual patterns fixed more on ideas and mental attitudes and accumulations of fact than on fully realized characters.

Benchley, Perelman, and Thurber especially, engineered a gentler, more character-driven style of satire that, among mainstream white audiences, made their versions of the Little Man enormously successful as new antiheroic images of American national character and the Great Good Place. Analysts of American humor argue that initially these audiences laughed *at* the Little Man (as they had at his lower-class cousin, Charlie Chaplin's "Little Tramp" from *Modern Times*) instead of *with* him, as had been the case with the craftier, more capable frontier types. Moreover, they laughed both with a feeling of *superiority* and with *surprise* (that anyone could be so gullible and so incompetent)—fulfilling two classic principles of comedy. But at the same time, the Little Man's audience could not help but be aware of the disconcerting parallels between his antic fears and frustrations and those of their own lives in an increasingly absurd and brutal world. By the 1950s the Little Man, and a cadre of like-minded comic antiheroes pioneered by the *New Yorker* magazine writers and their disciples, had become the dominant types in American humor; and what Thurber called "fables for our time"—*Is Sex Necessary?* (1929), *The Owl in the Attic and Other Perplexities* (1931), *The Middle-Aged Man on the Flying Trapeze* (1935), and *The Male Animal* (1940)—had become classics of urban American myth—grist for the comic mills of the "black humorists" and "fabulators" who reshaped American literary comedy and satire in the 1960s.

Kelley's characterizations in *dəm* adapt the fables of antiheroic comic white archetypes for his own time; and his own polemics on race matters in the months prior to *dəm*'s release specifically deploy the concept of the Little Man to clarify issues of race and class domination confronting the black freedom struggle. In an essay, "On Racism, Exploitation and the White Liberal," published by *Negro Digest* in January 1967, Kelley temporarily shed his artist's distaste for sociological problem solving long enough to draw what he believed was a crucial distinction between economic exploitation and racism. The two were often confused, he insisted, particularly in the minds of black integrationists and militant black separatists who, despite their opposing political strategies, were *both* bedeviled by the cult of whiteness. But whiteness, Kelley believed, was merely a highly elaborated *mystique* that throughout the history of white supremacy evolved mainly to rationalize the prior and more fundamental processes of economic exploitation. The notion, common to black leaders of either stripe, that "if we can force the white man to give up his racism, he will automatically cease to exploit us," Kelley maintained, "is a ridiculous idea" which ignores the reality that "to the true exploiter of American society, the Big White Man, race means nothing. He exploits his own as quickly, and with no more conscience, than he exploits black people. Who is more exploited," Kelley asked, "than a white Mississippian who dies in Vietnam defending an economic system that has given him nothing but a substandard education, a sharecrop farm, cheap clothes, and too little to eat?" As the personification of the American power elite at home and abroad, the Big White Man, Kelley continued, uses those who are by implication the Little White Men—both the middle-class White Liberal and the lower-class avowed White Racist—yes, to retard black progress, but more importantly to forestall any form of social change that requires what the Big White Man really sees as "his worst enemy": economic risk. Indeed, economic fear and insecurity, Kelley concludes, is the primary animus of conflict throughout the social structure, whether it concerns the lower-class white man (whose "fear is not that we will rape, or worse, marry his daughter, but that we will take his job") or the Little Man in the middle, the white liberal, who allies himself with blacks "not because he is committed to equality, but because the lower-class white is the one who most threatens his middle-class position in white American society."

This Little Man in the middle, updated to the age of Vance Packard's *Hidden Persuaders*, William Whyte's *Organization Man*, R. D. Laing's *Divided Self*, and the Vietnam War, is the comic and dramatic center around which the other characters in *dɔm* move, though Kelley's narrative, by social scientific extrapolation, ultimately transports his comic white antihero where the earlier *New Yorker* magazine writers never took him—away from his customary environs in the soft, white urban/suburban underbelly of John Wayne's America to the Harlem briar patch of one of Brer Rabbit's hipper, harder, street corner human counterparts. Kelley's Anglo protagonist is actually a Janus-faced, hybrid figure, part iconic war hero (Mitchell Pierce has served as a lieutenant in an unspecified Asian war), part Thurberian Little Man. The themes that Thurber had wrapped around the Little Man are still with him: the domestic blight and the trivia that eventually explode into major conflicts; the charged disjunction between childlike, daydreamy men and aggressive, pragmatic women; the lens on marriage as a state of undeclared war; the satiric narrative perspective that contrapuntally celebrates the natural, the individual, the subversive, over bourgeois social conventions and conformist systems of all sorts; and above all, the pervasive and provocative interplay of reality and fantasy. As one face of the dilemma of the modern American WASP, Mitchell Pierce is, however, modeled not so much on Thurber's Walter Mitty, who despite his general ineffectuality occasionally manages to dream and scheme his way to minor victories and a quixotic gallantry, but rather on those grimmer cases in the literary comedians' gallery of losers, whose fears and foibles so completely overwhelm them that they evoke the audience's shudder as often as a smile.

As such, Kelley's narcissistic Manhattan ad man bears an even stronger resemblance to the pathetic Mr. Monroe of Thurber's more cynical short stories in *The Owl in the Attic*, who "didn't really have any character. He had a certain charm, yes; but not character. He evaded difficult situations; he had no talent for firm resolution; he immolated badly; and he wasn't even very good at renunciation, except when he was tired or a little sick." Like Monroe, Mitchell Pierce visualizes himself in his daydreams as a masterful, romantic figure, when actually his life comprises a steady undercurrent of neurotic fixations and fears—of sidewalk panhandlers and imaginary muggers, of being displaced on his job, of social opprobrium, of sexual impotence. Even as an adulterer, when Mitchell Pierce plunges into a fantasy-spawned affair with a "working girl" soap opera actress, he is laughably ineffectual, like Mr. Monroe, and is rendered painfully more so by his shrewish wife's deprecating and all-knowing indifference.

Family life on this terrain of what Thurber called "stealthy doom" is a well-appointed wasteland, spiritually void, sensually impaired, combative. Children here are peripheral and annoying "pets," or worse, so that Pierce's wife, Tam, actually fears their young son, Jakie, and repeatedly "threatens" Mitchell with her pregnant belly of superfecundated twins. Tam's aggression toward Mitchell is untiring, businesslike, and pitiably ironic in the manner of some classic Thurber cartoons, like one that pictures a gargantuan woman reading a lurid romance novel, and who glances up coyly at her wimp of a husband and purrs, "it's our own story exactly! He bold as a hawk, she soft as the dawn." Another limns a huge harridan who coos, "Yoo-hoo, it's me and the ape man." Prey to wifely erotic fantasies, as is Mitchell Pierce, such males occasionally fight back with fantasies of their own—but lose, as does the Little Man in a Thurber tale who creates an escapist dream life so detached from reality that he is forced to choose between an insane asylum and the continued home care at the hands of a wife who "corrects" his every waking thought. The hapless neurotic chooses the "freedom" of the asylum over life with her but discovers that even there his fantasies are not free, since she visits him daily and corrects even the reported details of his nighttime dreams. Teased and tortured, on the one hand, by nagging, emotionally omnivorous wives who alternate psychic assaults with maleficent mothering, these child-men are bullied and badgered on the other by inevitable mothers-in-law who multiply their daughters' affronts to the Little Men's besieged masculinity with imperious demands, mother-daughter tag-team wheedling, and an ofttimes undisguised sexual innuendo that, as in the case of the Pierce mother-in-law, makes their daughters' mates seem incestuously married instead to them.

The wife and mother-in-law, however, are not the only female antitypes who people the family romance of the comic Anglo antihero. dəm also recasts another of the archetypal female foils of Thurber's Little Man: the comic, cantankerous, malaprop-spouting colored maid, whom Kelley converts into an axis of worm-turning events. Thurber's liberalism, like that of the other *New Yorker* satirists, was firmly constrained by his white middle-class angle of vision; and most of his neurotic white male and female characters are urbanites or suburbanites with hired help and summer cottages. In Thurber's fiction and in his autobiographical essays, he or his monied, book-learned persona wrangles routinely with "difficult" working-class servants, most often black maids, who strike the white man as "odd," cross-grained, stupid, or downright psychotic—and thereby convenient as butts of satire, or as foils for the educated, middle-class white neurotics. Kelley turns the tables on Mitchell Pierce by making Opal Simmons, the Pierce's emulative black maid and nanny, a register of her white employers' moral evasions and disproportion, as well as the ebony-skinned Trojan horse who brings the dark forces of chaos— in the form of her grudge-holding Harlem boyfriend, Cooley—into the Pierce household.

Our opening image of Mitchell Pierce comes through a grotesque and brutal encounter with a ragtag American Indian street beggar camped outside his front door. Mitchell mistakes the dozing panhandler for a pile of painter's rags and, in a lone demonstration of action-figure prowess, kicks him in the chest when the unfortunate Indian grabs Pierce's leg and asks for a dime. Nonetheless the author portrays his unseeing antihero as morally obtuse but *not* unsympathetic. Kelley had observed in the 1967 interview that "the really great writer is one who can make you feel sympathy" for malefactors; and he acknowledged that in his own work he likes "to create a character as a villain, and show something about him which will arouse sympathy." In *dəm*'s third section, "The Search for Love," where after a self-inflicted pratfall Mitchell Pierce convalesces in front of daytime television, he soon wanders blindly across the border between reality and soap opera fantasy. Kelley effects the transition through deft manipulations of point of view, moving the reader back and forth between a limited third-person omniscient scenario of Mitchell's own consciousness and a fabricated soap opera world manifested typographically by direct insertions of the TV screenplay—with directorial notes and character citations intact. The device creates a dramatic irony that enables us to empathize with Pierce even as we quickly understand what he does not—his disintegrating hold on the real world.

In Thurber's journalistic writing of the late 1940s, soap opera assumed the serious significance of a full-blown social syndrome; and in a five-part *New Yorker* series about radio soap operas, called "Soapland," Thurber sharply critiqued the "soap opera males" required by the plot patterns of this new mass media form of Americana. Dropping his comic mask for something close to psychoanalysis, he observed that male figures in soap opera were regularly afflicted with a variety of debilitating ailments—temporary blindness, amnesia, and temporary or permanent paralysis of the legs—that conversely made their good women "capable of twice as much work, sacrifice, fortitude, endurance, ingenuity, and love as before." Males rendered subordinate and dependent in Soapland are, he concluded, part of its symbolic logic: "as the psychologists put it, symbols that the listening women demand" from the "great American tradition of female domination." Thurber put the blame for this state of distorted reality not on women but on American men; and he discerned the ultimate consequences in a widening confusion of fiction with fact that manifested itself in the pathetic absurdity of soap opera listeners who thought that radio characters were *real* and sent in wedding or baby gifts when they got married or gave birth or who, after recognizing that Mister X, the husband in *Just Plain Bill*, and Mister Y, the husband in *Backstage Wife*, were played by the same actor, wrote indignantly to the studio that they were aware of this double life and threatened to expose the bigamy.

Like Thurber, Kelley finds soap opera a perfect satiric vehicle for underscoring the flight from reality to illusion, from responsibility to moral evasion; and like Thurber, Kelley associates the soap opera world with masculine displacement and infantilization. But where Thurber's perspective combined satire with an old romanticist faith in the redemptive powers of mature love and imagination, Kelley's fictional world is as emotionally bleak and unredeemable—at least for the Little Man—as the harshly surrealist nightmare environs of Thurber's less romantic and less popular contemporary Nathanael West, whom Kelley claims overtly as a major literary influence. During the 1930s West shared the same literary editor who shepherded Hughes's *The Ways of White Folks*; and S. J. Perelman, one of Thurber's *New Yorker* co-creators of the Little Man mythos, was his brother-in-law and literary confidante. But West's work thoroughly rejected the "muddle-class" realism Hughes had absorbed even from satirists of the middle class like

Sinclair Lewis and Mencken; and West deplored the tasteful, good-natured, whimsical tone characteristic of the *New Yorker* brand of Anglo-American humor. In a self-parodying advertisement for his own *The Dream Life of Balso Snell* (1931), West classed himself instead with the French: "In his use of the violently disassociated, the dehumanized marvelous, the deliberately criminal and imbecilic, he [West] is much like Guillaume Apollinaire, Jarry, Ribemont Dessaignes, Raymond Rousel, and certain of the surrealistes"—though, at the level of narrative devices, "a formal comparison with Lewis Carroll [is] possible."

A corollary comparison of West's fictional world with that of Kelley's *dəm* offers similar possibilities. Kelley's teacher, Hawkes, had associated West admiringly with a subterranean avant-garde tradition that ran from early Spanish and English picaresque novels, down through Lautreamont, Celine, Flannery O'Connor, and Nabokov, thence to his own generation of fabulators. The common thread, which Hawkes and Kelley now sought in their own creations, was "a quality of coldness, detachment, ruthless determination to face up to the enormities of ugliness and potential failure within ourselves and in the world around us, and to bring to this exposure a savage and saving comic spirit and the saving beauties of language." The ugliness and potential failure of the American Dream, seen from the depths of the Great Depression, had become West's special province; and he had pioneered the technically experimental, short "lyric novel" as a "distinct form" appropriate to an American environment where rootlessness, impoverishment, foreshortened family histories, and barren landscapes made epic conceptions obsolete. "Forget the epic, the master work," West had advised in some notes on *Miss Lonelyhearts* (1933), a novel conceived instead "in the form of a comic strip" in which "each chapter instead of going forward in time, also goes backward, forward, up and down in space like a picture" and in which "violent images are used to illustrate commonplace events . . . [and] left almost bald."

Like *The Dream Life of Balso Snell*, West's frenetic, scatological, and collagistic first novel, Kelley's *dəm* dissects the perversions of mass culture and the consumerist fantasies that Mitchell Pierce's ad agency produces to sell the "Heces" (read "feces") air deodorizer that underwrites the *Search for Love* soap opera which in turn anally envelops Pierce's psychic life. As in *Miss Lonelyhearts*, which is structured narratively to capture the spatial form and tempo of pop culture cartoon, and in which a male newspaperman with a Christ complex masquerades as a female advice columnist for the down and out, so in *dəm* the novel parodically recapitulates formulaic elements of soap opera melodrama: gossip and family scandal ballooned to grandiloquent import; false intimacy with characters who have fabricated personal histories but no psychic depth; links between story segments that cultivate a sense of serial installment; intentionally arrested plot development and teasing irresolution at the close. Like *A Cool Million*, in which West figuratively dismembers America's Horatio Alger myth of success, *dəm* shows that beneath the smooth material surface of middle-class prosperity lies a cauldron of repressed violence, racist xenophobia, and sexual dysfunction that manifests itself verbally in a procession of ethnic and sexual jokes and homicidally in the chillingly reasoned unreason of John Godwin, Mitchell Pierce's ad man workmate and nostalgic Marine Corps master of hand-to-hand mayhem. In "Some Notes on Violence," West had written wryly that "in America violence is idiomatic," so that unlike European authors American writers need not exhaustively explain the motivations for violence or prepare their audiences for it, since it has become a daily and constantly escalating dose of mass media titillation in their lives. So in *Day of the Locust* (1939), his apocalyptic satire about the Hollywood dream factory, when West aims his camera obscura at the losers on the fringes of "success," he reveals a whoring, sleazy place of illusion, where people with "two-dimensional faces that a talented child might have drawn with a ruler and a compass" come to manufacture synthetic dreams for others, and die in a riotous orgy of incendiary mob violence.

In West's horrific Hollywood, as in Kelley's Madison Avenue wasteland, the protagonist falls in love with the cardboard illusion represented by an archetypal blonde bitch goddess (Faye Greener in West's tale, Nancy Knickerbocker in Kelley's), in either case a whore turned actress who is all things to all men, completely artificial but so irresistible that, as West puts it, "nothing less than rape would do." In both incarnations, the fantasy woman is a "dream dreamed by all of America," on the silver screen or the soap opera television tube. She evokes no real personality but only a seductive and inherently amoral collage of cliches that, in

Day of the Locust provides "an invitation to struggle, hard and sharp, closer to murder than to love," and in the case of Mitchell Pierce's Winky Mendelblum/Nancy Knickerbocker, the maudlin "bathroom musak theme from *Search for Love*." Unlike the Great Gatsby's dream woman, however, neither of these two fantasy females has patrician allurements, no "tinkle of money in her voice," though Pierce's short-lived paramour has enough working girl savvy to play him off with soap-style repartee and a dose of shrill laughter as he retreats down her seedy hallway in a state of sickly sweet renunciation.

More than Fitzgerald, West, or Thurber, Kelley sets his comic antihero's adventures-in-fantasy against the backdrop of a succession of colliding ethnic subcontexts—WASP, Italian, Irish, Jewish, Cuban, and ultimately and most extensively, African American—though all are projected through a lens of satiric distortion. These symbolic ethnic contexts have a comic texture akin to that in *The Dream Life of Balso Snell*, where Balso meets a Jewish guide with "Tours" on the front of his cap, who proposes to lead the protagonist through the anal canal of Western civilization. From this excremental vantage point, all ethnic survival strategies are mired in the offal of consumerist exploitation and the corporate war machine; and ethnic chauvinism in all its guises becomes another form of grotesquerie, a species of comic con game that traffics in profitable stereotype and intracultural fratricide. After hailing a taxi ride from an all-American driver with "a pink, creased neck," for example, Mitchell spots a shrunken head with red hair hanging from the cab's rearview mirror and queries the driver about its origin. A veteran of WWII's South Pacific campaign against the Japanese, the driver nonchalantly relates a macabre tale of an island skirmish with "the Japs" in which he had taken advantage of a battlefield opportunity to liquidate his "dear old captain" (who had decided to "start a little slave-labor force with the natives"). After the skirmish, the captain's remains had mysteriously disappeared; but the mystery had been solved sometime later, on the next island, when a delegation of local head hunters presented a USO softball box to the cabby containing what appeared to be the captain's shrunken head, which subsequently enabled the perversely nostalgic driver to keep the grisly memento of his commanding officer "riding with [him] all these years."

What Nathan Scott, Jr., that most prolific and consciously theistic of African American literary critics, says of West's fictional devices might appropriately be said of such motifs in Kelley's dəm, that they are Kafka's *Amerika* "made even more nightmarish and bizarre as it is redone by an insider—whose penchant for a particular kind of joking makes for the very hard sort of objectivity belonging to satire." The particular kind of Kafkaesque joking in dəm was not an exclusively literary phenomenon at the time. In the late 1960s and early 70s as John Williams puts it, black militancy, black piety, black academic rationalism, black political realism, and black humor all existed side by side and were all converging on the system "in flank and frontal assaults." A new kind of black stage humor was emerging in the performances of older comedians like Redd Foxx and Slappy White, humor which jettisoned the ancient trappings and restraints of blackface minstrelsy and vaude- ville, along with the implicit compact that black jesters avoid wisecracks or "insolent" quips discomfiting to white audiences—hence Foxx's running gags about "uugggly white women" and White's targeted rips on random "white-bread" audience members. Mel Watkins suggests that at a time when the performative distance between black comics and white audiences was being erased and the public barriers were being challenged by integrated Freedom Rides and sit-ins and Black Power rallies, main- stream audiences were being primed for a satirical black voice "that mirrored the moral and ethical candor" of Martin Luther King, Jr., on the one hand, and Malcolm X on the other. Few of even the most virulent racists could still be amused or soothed by the servile postures and ingratiating tricksterism of old-time Negro humor when newspapers and broadcast television were bombarding them with images of thousands of blacks whose unsmiling clashes with fire hoses, police dogs, rabid white mobs, and brutish sheriffs eviscerated all those entrenched memories of Tambo and Bones, Uncle Tom, and Stepin Fetchit.

"A new brand of Negro comic" surfaced in 1967, Foxx asserted: one who was "clever, poised, informed, and tells it like it is." The charade was over—on the streets, on stage, and on the printed page; and a new dramatic voice for black satirists erupted onstage in the routines of humorists as different as Dick Gregory, Bill Cosby, and Richard Pryor: a voice which was not aggressive so much as uningratiating, not so much confrontative as unapologetic and self-assured. Among these, Pryor was the most unconventional and, as Steve Allen noted, the most literary, insofar as Pryor's stage comedy went beyond merely capturing comic glimpses of black street corner perceptions to creating an almost novelistic gallery of memorable and fully humanized black personality types. The literary qualities of Pryor's humor derived in part, John Williams suggests, from his mid 60s participation in a Bay area group of "hip, brash, talented, and tough" Black Arts writers and satirists that included former members of the New York-based Umbra Writers Workshop like Ishmael Reed and David Henderson, along with Cecil Brown (then at work on a satiric novel called *The Life and Loves of Mr. Jiveass Nigger*) and Claude Brown, the author of *Manchild in the Promised Land* (1965). Collectively, Williams recalls, they had a sense of humor, irony, and satire that often surpassed Pryor's; and they fused the styles of black vernacular humor with avant-garde absurdist, neo-surrealist, and metafictionist intellectual stances, resulting in raffish new fictional modes that some of their followers were calling "Black black humor." Reed, like Kelley and another black fabulator named Charles Wright, had originally been attracted to experimentalist satire also through an early introduction to the work of Nathanael West; and Reed would become the most controversial, the most prolific, and the most highly esteemed of the group. Through Pryor's role as one of the screenwriters for Mel Brooks's *Blazing Saddles,* motifs from Reed's two satiric "Neo-Hoodoo" Western novels, *The Freelance Pallbearers* (which debuted with Kelley's *dəm* in 1967) and *Yellow Back Radio Broke-Down* (1969), were pirated and perverted by Hollywood in ways that Reed, Kelley, and Wright, given their shared affinity for West's anal canal angle of vision on the dream factory, all knew were painfully predictable.

At the level of psychodynamics, what black performative humor like Pryor's shares with black literary satire is a race-conscious reworking of the "comic process" that Freud dissected in *Wit and Its Relation to the Unconscious*. Freud saw "joke-work" as a complex triangular relationship between the maker of a joke, the object of the joke, and the audience of the joke. While jokes themselves are a manifestation of the makers' aesthetic freedom to contemplate human affairs "playfully," their social power, Freud argued, lay in their joking ability to reveal to the audience something previously concealed, not by saying it outright but through indirection, double meaning, metaphorical compression, and deliberately ambiguous reasoning. Social affirmation of joke-work as art and as play, Freud theorized, depends on the audience maintaining "some degree of benevolence or a kind of neutrality, an absence of any factor that could provoke feelings opposed to the purpose of the joke," if the creative play of wit is to complete itself. He made a distinction between jokes that are "innocent" and have no purpose other than to give pleasure and those that have ulterior motives. Those with ulterior motives he called "tendentious" and categorized as either obscene or hostile. Obscene jokes create pleasure rooted in repressed acts of sexual aggression; hostile jokes derive their pleasure from the indirect defeat of perceived enemies: "By making our enemy small, inferior, despicable or comic, we achieve in a roundabout way the enjoyment of overcoming him."

In the 1960s the challenge for black comedians and satirists seeking "crossover" success was, as Watkins observes, to defuse the racial hostility and entrenched "us" versus "them" perspectives characteristic of segregated American society and of traditional ethnic jokes and humor. Unlike the old segregated black vaudeville and nightclub circuit, in which the comedy largely excluded whites by concentrating on black insider humor or by making "them" the object of satire, the new brand of civil rights era comedy had to include crossover audiences in the "joke-work" enough to establish a shared perspective on the object of the joke, or an acceptable balance between racial targets. Dick Gregory concluded that, when "comfortable and secure" on their own turf, white audiences had no inclination to laugh at "racial material they didn't want to hear"; and he recognized that, when on their turf, "I've got to make jokes about myself, before I can make jokes about them and their society." Wright's satiric near future fantasy novel, *The Wig: A Mirror Image*, published the year before *dəm*, in 1966, develops a literary analogue of Gregory's strategy, in a fabulative satire that led the *New York Times* to pronounce its author "the first certified Negro black humorist." Set in "an America of tomorrow," *The Wig* recounts the tale of a twenty-one-year-old light-skinned Harlemite who is determined to live the American Dream, and who Silky Smooths his hair in the delusive hope that his pomaded "wig" will magically jet him to the Great Society goal of "pretty girls, credit cards, charge accounts, Hart Schaffner & Marx suits, fine shores, Dobbs hats, XK-E Jaguars, and more pretty girls." His mirrored image reflects, "in an occult fashion, a magnificent future"; but in his "butterscotch-colored dreams" he is "Walter Mitty's target-colored stepson," and headed for disaster:

> A politician had prophesied that it was extremely likely a Negro would be elected President of the United States in the year 2000. Being realistic, I could just picture myself as Chairman of the Handyman's Union, addressing the Committee on Foreign Relations and then being castrated. At least I'd no longer have to phone Mr. Fishback, the necrophilic funeral director, each time I went downtown. What a relief that would be. The dimes I'd save.

Enthralled with his own "all-American girl"—a mercenary black prostitute with her own wig fixations—he takes a job for a Southern-fried chicken restaurant, crawling around Manhattan in a yardbird suit with electrified feathers to win her "love" and finance her addictions, until he learns that his fair lady, "The Deb," has been summarily run over by a school bus. Indeed, the book ends in mocking self-debasement and the prophesied emasculation of the butterscotch-colored stepson of Thurber's Little Man, whom Wright has thrown here out of the Great Good Place into West's American nightmare. Reed called *The Wig* "one of the most underrated novels written by a black person in this century"; but Wright himself came to consider the book a "retarded child," mired in authorial uncertainty and consequent audience ambivalence.

Kelley seeks an uncluttered comic vision in dəm, and a less ambiguous relationship with his intended audience. Mitchell Pierce's antagonist, the black anti-antihero, Calvin Coolidge Williams ("Cooley"), is prepared to turn the other cheek on Mister Charlie's world—but that cheek is gluteal, not mandibular. If our analogy between black literary satirists and stage performers holds, Kelley's approach to joke-work and the comic process is closer to Pryor's than to Gregory's. Gregory had carefully analyzed the untoward relationship between the black jokester whose material pillories white racism and white audiences whom the jokester is enjoined to entertain; and Gregory had worked out his own performative answer to the potentially disastrous complex of white anxiety, guilt, and repressed rage or hate. Pryor had discovered yet another strategy—hyperbolic, vitriolic, unsparing, congenitally scatological, yet caustically humane. John Williams's son and coauthor, Denis, suggests in an afterthought to their joint study of Pryor's tragicomic career that Pryor spoke directly to "us" [black folks, that is] "in our native language—there was no mistaking that—but he did it in a way that was slyly accessible to any white who dared eavesdrop. He was telling 'them' off and taking them to school even as he taught and entertained us."

Pryor routines like "Whitefolks" and "Shortage of White Folks," for example, parallel *dəm*'s delicate balance of hostility and neutrality toward the object of the jokes, of revelation and comic recrimination toward the audience. Like Pryor's riffing performances, the "particular kind of joking" that frames the action of *dəm* marks its novelistic world off as a domain of hyperbolized symbolic inversion, a betwixt-and-between cultural space where the "official" world of sociocultural power relations is symbolically dismembered, disrupted, reduced to chaos; and it is a world of thwarted sexual desire and pandemic victimization that seems incapable of being fully righted and reordered, for either the white folks who hold power or the black folks who must somehow endure and live to love and laugh another day. As a self-conscious work of written literature, of course, *dəm* moves beyond the tight constraints of live comedy performance to construct, at another level, a set of complex joking relationships with the literary canon, and with anticanonical allies. All of Kelley's other novels employ titles that play with canonical icons: *A Different Drummer* with Henry Thoreau's *Walden*; *Dancers on the Shore* with Joseph Conrad's *Heart of Darkness*; *A Drop of Patience* with Shakespeare's *Othello*; *Dunsfords Travels Everywheres* with James Joyce's *Finnegans Wake*. In *dəm*, clusters of allusion make Mitchell Pierce's search for his wife's second fecundator seem like a parody of the protagonist's underground trip to Harlem in Ellison's *Invisible Man*. The cross-racial sexual triangle between Mitchell, Tam, and Cooley appears in some ways to have consciously given a mojo twist to a similar triangle of problematic paternity and race-mixing involving Skipper, Sonny, and Catalina Kate in Hawkes's *Second Skin*. And by a startling symbolic serendipity—since Kelley somehow never read Genet's *The Blacks* or saw it staged—the recurring imagery and symbols associated with the principal white characters in *dəm* replicates the archetypal signifiers of destructive racial and matriarchal power that Genet deployed to surrealistic effect in the dramaturgy of *The Blacks*. The opening scene of Mitchell Pierce stomping the ragtag Indian panhandler seems to recast jokingly the stomping and murder of a ragbag Paris street hag by one of the unmasked black principals in *The Blacks*. The role of the cuckolded white husband of the seduced and murdered blonde in Genet's metadrama doubles as the mythic starting point for Mitchell Pierce's comically blind travail in Kelley's less sinister but no less ominous tale. And the wig, balls of yarn, and knitting needles that make up the transvestite representation of the white bitch goddess in *The Blacks* reappear as Tamara Pierce's archetypal accoutrements in *dəm*.

dəm is, after all, by its own defiantly mythopoetic title, an excursion into self-reflexive otherness—as seen through the style and logic of a particular linguistic universe. Clarence Major, another of the Black Arts experimental novelist fabulators who developed conceptual interests in the lexical and syntactic worldview of African American communities, notated "dem" in his 1970 New Breed dictionary of Afro-American slang, as a *deliberate* corruption of "them," dating back to the turn of the sixteenth century, which refers specifically to white people. The term in fact occurs throughout the English-speaking New World black diaspora as a pan-creole catchword for the *buckra*, the *ofay*. As in many parts of West Africa, it uses the demonstrative pronoun as a single form for subject, object, and possessive cases, and "when placed in front of a proper name, denotes the group to which the person concerned is thought of as belonging." Yet, in its Euro-American usages, it also became a vernacular variation on the all purpose profanity, "damn" or "demn," so that, in the end, it fuses otherness with damnation in an willfully comic deformation of the King's English. A devilish way to hook us on a fable.

His dream must have seemed so close that he could hardly fail to grasp it. He did not know that it was already behind him, somewhere back in that vast obscurity beyond the city, where the dark fields of the republic rolled on under the night.

F. Scott Fitzgerald, *The Great Gatsby*

The ruin of a nation begins in the homes of its people.

Ashanti proverb

Note:

Superfecundation is the fertilization of two ova within a short period of time by spermatozoa from separate copulations. It is only distinguishable from usual two-egg twinning if the female has coitus with two males with diverse physical characters, each passing his respective traits to the particular twin he has fathered.

Alan F. Guttmacher, *Pregnancy and Birth*

CONTENTS

næʊ, ləmi təljə hæʊ dəm foks lɪv . . .

WHEN JOHNNY...

1

Someone, thought Mitchell Pierce, is having his apartment painted. A large pile of painter's rags—what looked like a spotted gray tarp, an old Indian blanket, a black unblocked fedora—sat on the pavement just outside the front door of his apartment building. In the June morning heat, steam rose from the rags. Mitchell walked from under the awning, stopped, felt a lukewarm sun on his shoulder, and wondered why he was not beginning to sweat. Then a hand grabbed his ankle.

"You got a dime, chief?" Under the black hat, the Indian smiled with only one side of his mouth; the other side held a cigar. Now Mitchell could smell him, sweet and pungent as old bananas. "Come on, chief, a few silver trinkets."

Mitchell tried to pull his leg free, but the Indian held fast, red and black eyes staring from a broad brick-colored face cut by a thousand tiny wrinkles, coated with soot, caged by two thick braids. Breakfast, not long crushed, began to turn in Mitchell's stomach. He put his foot into the Indian's chest and tried to kick him away.

"Just a dime, chief, so I can make the happy hunting grounds."

Pulling change from his pocket, Mitchell aimed at the Indian's face; the hand left his ankle. Late already, he did not wait for a thank you. At the office, his stomach still upset, he was told by his secretary that Mr. Cook wanted to see him immediately.

He knew why. Mr. Cook had assigned Mitchell and a coworker, John Godwin, a commercial. Since Mitchell knew very little about the intricacies of selling such a product, Godwin had volunteered to do it alone, and Mitchell had agreed. He had seen Godwin's work only minutes before they submitted it to Mr. Cook. But those few minutes had been enough. Even Mitchell knew it was a bad job. Now he would have to face Mr. Cook, and accept half the responsibility for the failure, or confess that he had done no work at all.

Mr. Cook's office did not have a desk, only fifteen orange leather chairs, arranged into three circles in various parts of the room. They sat in the chairs nearest the window, the sun just outside, above the river, Mr.

Cook's back to the window. Mitchell was glad to be squinting. It would be harder for Mr. Cook to know what he was thinking.

"I'm not going to ask which of you fellows is basically responsible. I think I know already. Besides, the last thing I want is a spy system around here." Mr. Cook, eyes shaded by yellow-tinted spectacles, smiled at Mitchell and John Godwin in turn; the sun lit his thinning hair from behind. "All I care about is creating a one-minute play that will educate people about their need for HECES. So maybe if we sit here and work on it together, we can get something by lunchtime. All right?"

Mitchell had just torn out a match, the cigaret already between his lips, when Mr. Cook asked the question. He answered as quickly as he could: "Yes, sir." Godwin simply nodded and Mitchell wondered if ever he would have that kind of courage.

Mr. Cook did not seem to notice. "Now, we have this couple, in their early thirties. Two ugly people. The husband is balding. The wife? No hairdo. Straight hair, brown, a little curl on the end. Am I right? Those are the kind of people who buy HECES. What're they wearing?" He smoothed his tie, and waited.

Godwin, to Mitchell's right, crossed his legs. "What time of day is it?"

"You're supposed to be telling me, John."

"I thought you might want to change it." Godwin looked at Mitchell for a second. "We put the time in the early evening, after supper."

"All right. Now, what're they wearing?"

Godwin turned to Mitchell. "I think you have some ideas on that."

This was not true; he rephrased what Mr. Cook had already said. "Well, sir, I saw them as working people. The wife has on a cheap housedress. The husband has on a white shirt, with his sleeves rolled up."

Mr. Cook was happy, but did not smile. "Now look what you have here? The man says: *Gee, honey, this room smells really good tonight. Did you use some air freshener?* And she says: *No, I used HECES.* And then you go into the demonstration and the rest of it. It's all wrong. Awareness of a problem must come before a person begins to look for an answer to that problem. Those people aren't that smart. You see what I mean?"

Mitchell was not sure, but nodded anyway.

Godwin lit a cigaret, exhaled, looking out of the window.

Mr. Cook sighed. "Now, do you have any suggestions?" He sat back in his chair, his thumb and index finger starting at the tip of his nose and sliding up, under the two yellow circles to press against his closed eyes.

Godwin signaled Mitchell to lead off.

Mitchell doubted that Godwin was actually giving him the opportunity to answer the question. More likely, he was trying to get Mitchell to test out Mr. Cook. Then Godwin could judge Mr. Cook's reaction and make his own suggestion. But he decided to gamble and accept the challenge. "Well, sir, it seems to me that we must make people aware of their fears." Mr. Cook nodded. "And don't people fear rejection most of all?"

"Right." Mr. Cook came forward in his chair. "Go on."

He glanced at Godwin, who, surprisingly enough, seemed genuinely pleased. "So we can start with silence, no music, just these two ugly people sitting in their living room. We have a close-up of the husband, balding, needing a shave, an ape. Then his wife, plain as a grocery bag. They're sitting in the living room, just staring at each other. Their life is boring and dull. They're lonely. Then the husband says: *Gee, honey, I wonder why no one ever comes to visit us?*"

"Good, Mitchell." Mr. Cook smiled at Godwin, who nodded as if Mitchell were his younger brother, though they knew each other only slightly. "Then what does the wife say?" Mr. Cook had stopped smiling.

Mitchell tried several answers to himself, but none seemed right. The room was very quiet.

"Something like: *The Jensens always have a house full of friends.* Right, Mitchell?" Godwin was trying to help him; Mitchell could not understand why.

"All right, John." Mr. Cook frowned. "But that doesn't really advance the action. We have the rejection theme started. We have to keep it moving."

Godwin nodded, did not defend himself.

But Godwin had given Mitchell time, and he thought he had the answer, and even decided to risk coming to Godwin's aid. "Excuse me, Mr. Cook, but I think John is trying to give us a second for reflection. I may be wrong—I mean, you'd probably know better—but I wouldn't rush them. Let this new awareness of their loneliness sink in."

Mr. Cook thought for a moment. Godwin seemed to be watching a bird, wings sparkling, circle away toward the river.

"All right, Mitchell. I'll accept that. But then what?"

"Then the husband says: *You know, I've been hearing about something new, called* HECES. Then he tells a little bit about it . . ."

But Mr. Cook was shaking his head. "No, Mitchell. You've made a mistake. The wife's got to get the idea. She's the one who does all the buying. She's the one who watches television all day."

"You meant wife, didn't you, Mitchell?" The bird had disappeared and Godwin had returned to them.

Surprised again, but picking up his cue, Mitchell made himself laugh. "Did I say husband? I'm sorry, sir. I mean wife." He watched, but could not tell if Mr. Cook believed him.

"All right, the rest is easy. The demonstration. Then what?" Mr. Cook smiled at them. "I want you fellows to earn your money."

"The obvious stuff, Mr. Cook." Godwin sat up. "We give the husband a good shave, a suit coat, and a tie. The wife gets a nice simple hairdo, not too much to notice, and a cocktail dress with some spangles on it. We change the lighting. And a house full of people, a party setup, some music, and couples dancing in the background. The husband kisses the wife, and says: *Gee, honey, I'm sure glad you made me get some* HECES. That what you had in mind, Mitchell?"

He nodded.

"All right then. When can I see a final draft with camera directions?"

"In a week, Mitchell?" Godwin crushed out a cigaret and started to get up.

"I think so." Mitchell gathered his notes.

Mr. Cook walked to the door between them. "I always have a better lunch when I know I've done a good morning's work. What about you fellows?"

He and Godwin agreed.

They walked the two flights down to their offices, Mitchell following. Godwin held the door for him. "It was nice of you not to say I messed up the assignment, Mitchell. My mind isn't within a million miles of here."

WILLIAM MELVIN KELLEY

"What about you?" Mitchell was still puzzled. "You kept throwing me fat pitches."

"Why not?" Godwin shrugged. "Listen, how about lunch? You have anything on?"

"No." Mitchell shook his head. "Sure, let's have lunch."

2

They met in the lobby of their building, near the cripple's newsstand, and walked out into the street. Most of the millions of secretaries — in short cotton dresses, under shining helmetlike hair — were already hurrying back to their offices.

At the corner, a yellow taxi and a blue sedan had collided. The two drivers, a neckless Italian and a balding man, his white arms sticking from rolled-up plaid sleeves, stood in shattered glass shouting threats. Godwin wanted to watch, but Mitchell had a three-thirty appointment.

"That's the third one I've seen this week." Godwin stopped again to light a cigaret. "Listen, Mitchell, I'm really sorry you had to share the blame for that mess."

Despite all that had happened, Mitchell had been expecting an hour of excuses. Now he wondered why Godwin had wanted this lunch. "We haven't got very much to do now." He pulled open the thick glass door of the restaurant, and began to shiver.

Godwin dropped his cigaret, twisted it apart with his right toe.

They sat in a back booth and waited for their drinks. Godwin lit another cigaret. "You were in the last Asian war, weren't you?"

"That's right." Mitchell waited, a habit. Whenever someone began a new conversation, it was best to see how it developed before joining it.

"So was I." Godwin exhaled. "Marine Corps. I was just out of college when it started and I wanted to toughen myself up." He thought a moment. "And I guess I did."

Godwin did not look or talk like a Marine. He was tall, thin, gaunt even, with hands too small for his long arms, and almost shaggy hair. In meetings, he did not say much, did not seem very ambitious.

Their drinks came and they ordered lunch.

"My mind wasn't on that piece at all, Mitchell. The Marine Corps is calling me up."

"No kidding? Asia again?"

"I guess so." He shook his head, smiling. "It was a real surprise. I didn't think they'd need the old men for this one."

"I'm sorry, John."

The waiter arrived with their lunch—for Mitchell, a steak ringed by hard little potatoes; for Godwin, lamb chops and spinach. They each ordered another drink, pausing in their conversation until the waiter, too attentive, had left them.

Because there was no particular rivalry between them, and because of Godwin's conduct that morning, Mitchell offered honest sympathy. "I really don't think you'll have to worry about your position, John. They give leaves of absence. Naughton got called up last year and there didn't seem—"

Godwin's arm waved his small hand. "Sure, sure, if they want me back, I'll be back."

Mitchell could feel his brain swelling with alcohol. "No, I don't think you have to worry."

With metal tools, Godwin carved the meat away from the bone, which he picked up in his fingers. "I don't think you understand, Mitchell. I liked the Corps."

"Liked it?" Mitchell used his broadest smile.

"I'm serious." Godwin's eyes were blue. He did not continue, instead, lowered his mouth to his bone. "Is there a good hardware store around here?"

Mitchell did not know. He was still thinking about the way Godwin had looked at him.

"My power mower's broken. I have to get a part for it." He shrugged. "Well, I didn't feel like mowing the lawn this weekend anyway."

Mitchell had been enjoying his steak. Very carefully he had separated the rim of fat from the lean red meat and pushed it to the side of his plate, wishing he could hide the fat somewhere. "How do you like it out there?"

"It's wonderful. Especially for the kids. Before we moved, my boy was always losing fights. But since we've been out there, he's gotten much tougher. He can really take care of himself." Finishing his bone, Godwin cleaned his hands. His napkin looked like shredded waxed paper. "I don't go for all the stuff the Marine Corps dishes out, but a kid does have to know how to handle himself. At least they taught me that. You know anything about the Marines?"

"Not much." Mitchell's throat was dry; he looked for the waiter.

"Well, every man in the Corps is essentially a rifleman. Then they teach you a specialty. It can be cooking, or radio, or killing by hand. That's my specialty. I know seventy different ways to kill with my bare hands. Scares me sometimes, knowing how to do that. But at least I can walk through that God-damned park without being afraid."

Mitchell envied that. Sometimes on Saturday mornings, he would put Jake, his baby son, in his carriage and push him through the park. Whenever he passed a Black man, his heart would knock under his coat. He would walk on, hoping the Black man was not following him. For a moment, he looked at Godwin's small hands. "You ever do it?"

Godwin nodded. "About thirty times, I guess. I used to go on a lot of missions behind enemy lines."

"I had some combat duty, but it was the usual stuff, shooting at a bush or a rock. I don't think I ever saw one of them."

"I saw plenty, usually from behind." He leaned forward, his hands around his almost empty glass. "You have to be quiet. You blacken your face and move as quiet as a butterfly." He smiled. "Cover the scream, break the windpipe. You want any dessert?"

"No, thanks. How does it make you feel?"

"Feel? You don't feel anything. Most of the time you get yourself something, like morphine." He turned the right side of his head toward Mitchell. "You ever take a close look at my ear?"

For the first time, Mitchell saw the little hole. Godwin had a pierced ear. "One time I got so high I did that." He pinched the lobe. "You numb it, and jam in a needle. I used to wear a little gold ring. But Cindy didn't like it. I guess I would've looked funny as hell in the office with an earring. But lots of men did it. It was kind of hard to take out my earring and come back to work."

Mitchell understood this. In Asia, he had once gone six months without a bath. Back home, he found he had almost forgotten how to knot a tie.

"I guess I'll be putting in my earring again." Godwin sat up and raised his arm. When the waiter came, they each ordered another drink and did not speak until they arrived. Mitchell spent the time imagining how he would look with an earring.

"You know, Mitchell, one of these Sundays you have to come out. You like baseball?"

Mitchell nodded.

"We could sit around and watch the ball game and get a little drunk. We could make a stand. Order the wives to drive the kids over to the woods and we could just sit."

"Nice. That'd be nice, John."

"The neighborhood's getting quiet now. All the wives and kids're going away for the summer. We could just sit and watch a double-header. But I guess you'll have to make it soon." Godwin was rocking from side to side. "You know what I liked about the Marine Corps. You didn't have to pussyfoot around. You killed or screwed anything yellow and talked to anything white. It was simple."

Mitchell remembered how wary he had been in the conference with Mr. Cook, continued his thought aloud. "You don't have to wait and see what anybody's going to say. You just come out and talk."

Godwin had not been listening. "You get yourself one of those little yellow girls, keep her in food, and you have a very, very good friend." He let his fist fall onto the table. "And no back talk!"

In Asia, Mitchell had kept a friend like that. She had even unslanted her eyes for him.

Suddenly, Godwin started to laugh. "You ever hear that joke about the young correspondent who was going to relieve an old correspondent in Hong Kong? For hours, they sit in the editor's office and talk about the political situation, the economic situation, the important contacts. But when they come out of the editor's office, the young one says to the old one: 'That's all very interesting, George, but that isn't what I want to know. Let me ask you one thing. You know what they say about Oriental women, about how they're built? Does it really run crossways?' The old one just looks at him. 'Did you really believe that nonsense? Of course, it doesn't run crossways. But I'll tell you one thing: an hour after you're finished, you're as hungry as hell!'"

Both men began to giggle, their hands over their mouths.

"Really? 'You're as hungry as hell!'" Mitchell repeated the punch line.

They paid their checks and left the restaurant. Mitchell, in a good mood, was still laughing at the joke. Avoiding the sun, they walked in the cool shadow of the buildings.

"Remember what I was talking about before, about you coming out to see me? Why not this Sunday?" Godwin's blue eyes seemed darker now.

"Well, I can't tell you for sure. Tam might have something planned. But I'll phone her and let you know before we leave the office today."

Godwin nodded. "Push it, boy. We got to make a stand."

3

Mitchell had hesitated to accept Godwin's invitation, not because he had to consult his wife (he knew already Tam had nothing planned for Sunday), but because he did not quite understand why Godwin had asked him to visit. After his three-thirty appointment, he spent the last hour of the afternoon trying to figure it out. He and Godwin had never been friendly, had lunched together only when business made it necessary. Perhaps, Godwin now wanted to make Mitchell a friend, to protect himself. It had been, after all, a very poor script. Or perhaps Godwin wanted someone in the firm to watch over his interests while he was in Asia. Then the invitation could even have been a simple gesture of friendship, though Mitchell doubted it. Unable, finally, to decide what Godwin was planning, Mitchell based the decision on his own feelings. He realized then that he admired Godwin, not just for his ability to walk through the park unafraid, but because of the way he handled himself with Mr. Cook. Godwin's fearlessness might spring from nothing more than the knowledge that he was leaving the firm, or it might grow from something deeper. Mitchell decided he wanted to know for certain, and accepted Godwin's invitation. He told Tam that evening, just as they were stepping out of their slippers.

"Oh, Mitchell, why didn't you make it for next Sunday?"

He was punching his pillow, wondering if they needed a thin blanket to shield them from the air conditioner. "You weren't planning anything, were you?"

"No, I mean, not to do anything." He was not looking at her, but could hear her fanning the pages of a magazine. "But we could've just stayed home."

He rolled toward her. "Where were you this afternoon?"

"I had my hair done." Her hair was dark, shineless, recently cut short where jaw joined cheek, and parted on the right side.

"I tried to get you all afternoon." He lied. "Finally, I just had to give him an answer. I didn't know you'd get so upset." They could just as well stay home the following Sunday. "Listen, Tam, John Godwin is a good man to be friendly with. He's been with the firm much longer than I have."

She opened the magazine to a picture of a thin girl in a flowered slip. "I'll tell Opal to come and baby-sit."

He rolled away from her, certain that even in the lighted room, his lids would supply more than enough darkness for sleep. But after five minutes, he realized he could not keep his eyes closed, and rolled toward her again. "I can't sleep."

She was no longer reading. The magazine lay closed in her lap. "You have some pills in the bathroom." She did not look at him.

He shook his head, crunching his hair against the pillow. "Then I'll be groggy all day tomorrow."

She shrugged. The light was behind her; the line of her profile was darker than her face. The tip of her nose was a dime-sized ball. He watched her raise her cigaret, the smoke coming out through puckered lips in a thin stream. Under the covers, he inched his hand toward her side.

"That tickles."

"Relax and it'll feel sexy."

She pushed his hand away. "Stop, Mitchell, that tickles!" Turning toward him, she blew smoke into his eyes. "Besides, I'm not a sleeping pill." She did not smile, but he could not believe she was serious.

"I know that, Tam."

"Then don't." Her face softened. "Anyway, I haven't got in my stopper."

He smiled. "Well, why don't you trot into the bathroom and put it in."

She stared at him. "You really want me to?"

"I don't want to force you." He paused. "But it is your job."

"God, I wish you wouldn't say things like that." She took another drag on her cigaret. "But I guess it is." Sighing, she put her feet on the floor. "All right."

It seemed to take her a long time, but finally she returned, snapped off the lamp, slid into bed, and put her arms around his neck. "You know I love you, don't you, Mitchell?" She sounded just the slightest bit worried.

"Sure." He patted her back. Through her nightgown, her skin was cold.

"I mean, I hope you don't think I didn't want to make love to you.

WILLIAM MELVIN KELLEY

I mean, I always do, anytime you ask me to."

He laughed softly. "Anytime?"

"Yes, really." She kissed him hard, pushing his head deep into the pillow, so that it curled around his ears like a close-fitting cap. She was half on top of him. But suddenly, she withdrew her lips, squinting down at him in the light from the street below. "Is anything wrong?"

He could just hear her through the pillow. "What?" He lifted his head.

"You're not doing anything." She rolled away, onto her back. "You're just lying there."

He propped himself on his elbow, facing her. "No, I'm not, Tam." Shaking his head, he wondered what she wanted him to do.

"Nothing was happening to you." She was sulking. "I could tell."

He tried to make a joke of it. "How do you know what's happening to me?"

"I couldn't feel anything."

That was true, he supposed. "But we just started."

"I started on my way to the bathroom." Then she added, almost timidly. "If you know what I mean."

He put his hand on her stomach. The baby had been born almost a year before, but still she had not done the exercises prescribed by the doctor. "Of course. I feel the same way."

"Well, what's wrong? Don't I please you anymore?"

"Now you're being silly." He tried to keep the anger out of his whisper. He wanted to make love and get some sleep.

"Something's wrong." She slid toward the head of the bed, was almost sitting up now, half out of the sheet. "Did you bring your cigarets in here?"

"Yes." He grabbed her around the waist and began to tug her back down to him. "But you haven't got time."

They went on with it. But Mitchell had to think about the girl who had unslanted her eyes for him when he was fighting in Asia.

4

They were in their car by one Sunday afternoon, driving uptown beside the park, through Harlem — windows tight, the car air-conditioned, fearful at each stoplight — and, after crossing the last bridge on the east side of the island, caught the highway to Westchester. Mitchell told Tam to roll down her window and breathe some clean country air.

"Did this Godwin give you directions?" Her knees were clamped together where they emerged from her bright pink skirt.

"Come on, Tam. Why don't you want to meet him?"

"I didn't say that."

"What's wrong with you then?" Mitchell moved to the left and overtook a convertible, top down, driven by a white boy with a beard of scars and pimples. A girl sat beside him, her elaborate black hair kerchiefed against the wind, her arm around his neck. When Mitchell came abreast of them, she pointed, and began to shout into the boy's ear. In a few seconds, the boy had caught up and was leering into their car.

Tam, who had been preparing her answer, did not notice. "I hate to nag, really I do. But I don't think it was fair of you to make this date without telling me."

"I tried to call you." Beyond her, the boy was yelling at them, but the wind carried his words away, and Mitchell could not read lips. The convertible moved closer; Tam could have reached out and stroked the boy's enflamed cheeks.

"I know you did, Mitchell, and . . . all right. But then you could've waited until you got home." She held tightly to a small straw purse in her pink lap.

"Hey, you bastard! Hey!" The girl had taken the wheel now; the boy had jumped onto the seat, and stretched across the inches that separated his car from Mitchell's, his hands on their windowsill. "Hey, big man, this is my road. Nobody passes Ricco McInerney on his road. Ain't that right, baby?" He leaned into their car and tried to kiss Tam, who moved to the middle of the seat.

Mitchell stepped on the gas. But the girl was a good driver and stayed with him.

"Hey, Marilyn, give them a bump." Ricco McInerney shouted over his shoulder, but did not release Mitchell's car. Marilyn edged another foot closer, fender against fender. Mitchell's left-side tires scraped the low concrete rim of the roadway. He put on his brakes.

But Ricco McInerney had been watching Mitchell's foot, and pulled his hands away before he could be dragged out of his car.

"Stop, Mitchell." Tam was grabbing his sleeve. "Just stop and let them go."

He shook her away. "I didn't start this." He waited for Marilyn to slow down, but she did not. Before Mitchell could catch up, the convertible had turned off the highway, Ricco McInerney standing, looking back, sticking out his tongue at them.

Mitchell did not speak to Tam for another ten minutes, not until they too had left the highway. Then he reached into his pocket and handed her the directions Godwin had written for him. "Read those to me, will you, please?"

"Can't we make up before we get there, Mitchell?" She was whining.

"Sure, but read the directions first."

She did, and while he was searching for street signs, began again to explain herself. "It's just that when you don't even ask me, I feel left out. I begin to think you don't care about me or my feelings."

"Don't be silly." Most of the signs were hidden by the leaves of the roadside trees, as if the people living in that community did not want themselves found. "I tried to explain it to you. If I know for a fact that you don't have something planned, what good reason can you give me to call and ask you if you do have something planned? Doesn't that make sense?"

He was speeding, slowing, speeding the car, scouting for signposts at each corner. Beside him, Tam lurched forward and back. "Of course, Mitchell." She sighed. "I'm talking about how it makes me feel to be left out."

"Okay, we'll talk about how you feel. Don't you see, it's silly of you to feel that way? If I knew you had something planned, you know I wouldn't plan anything."

She shrugged, clamping her upper-arms against her ribs. "But I kind of did have something planned. We could've—"

"Yes, yes, I know. We could've just stayed home." He found Godwin's street and, without braking, turned left, throwing Tam against the door. "And done what? Watched television? You don't like to watch television."

Shrugging again, she lowered her head, the skin pulling tight over the tiny round bone at the top of her spine. "I guess you're right."

"Of course, I'm right. But that's not really the point." He took a deep breath, his eye on the house numbers. "All I'm trying to say is that you shouldn't get upset about things that don't matter very much."

"But I'm different from you." Staring ahead, her face was all but hidden by her straight brown hair. "I get upset about different things. What's silly to you is sometimes very important to me . . ." She stopped, thought. "Maybe just because I'm a woman?"

Reluctantly, Mitchell pulled to the curb and, leaving the motor running, shifted into Park. He was within two-hundred numbers of Godwin's house, and he wanted all this settled before he reached it. "That may be the most stupid and hypocritical thing you've ever said. If I actually treated you like a woman, I wouldn't consult you at all. I'm trying to treat you like a reasoning human being!"

She ran her index finger through the dust on the leather dashboard. "I know that, Mitchell, but . . ."

"But what? Most of the time you talk about how bad men are to women, then you turn around and want some kind of special treatment because you *are* a woman. I mean, God, make up your mind."

"All right, Mitchell." She nodded. "What time is he expecting us?"

"Two." He moved slowly on down the street, looking for Godwin's stone house.

5

Godwin was on the front lawn, behind his power mower, pins of grass spraying around his ankles. He did not look up until Tam had slammed her door. Then he reined in the mower only for a moment—raising a hand hidden in a white work glove, smiling—before he returned to his work. Except for the gloves, he was dressed as if about to leave for the city, in a dark summer suit, a dark tie, a white shirt buttoned to the collar. A spot of sun twinkled on his earlobe.

He had already finished the half of the lawn nearest the house. The grass was cut so short that it shone like a pool. They stood on the fieldstone walk and watched the mower pull him toward a high hedge that separated his property from his neighbor's, and back to them. "Hello, Mitchell. Is this your wife?"

Before Mitchell could answer, he turned away, beginning a new row. Mitchell started after him. "You got it fixed, huh?"

Godwin shook his head. "That's why the grass is flying all over the place. I'll have to rake it up later."

They had to shout over the sputtering motor.

"Your wife inside, John?" They had reached the hedge.

"We had a fight. She's riding around somewhere. She does that when she gets mad. I got jumpy waiting, so I decided to do some work. Might as well finish now."

"Sure." Mitchell peeked through the hedge into the next yard. Several people sat in steel chairs, around a white steel table. There was a bottle, square and half-empty, and several bowls of potato chips in its center. The people drank and stared at each other.

"I'll be finished in a couple of minutes. Why don't you go inside and fix yourselves a drink."

"Okay." When they reached the walk, Mitchell left Godwin, took Tam's elbow, and led her toward the house.

"What's wrong with him?" she whispered.

He pressed the latch with his thumb, pushed open the door. "He and his wife had a fight. He wants to work it off." Smiling, he wished that sometimes he too had a lawn to mow.

He closed the door behind them, watching to see if Tam was impressed with the house, but could not tell. The living room was to the left of the front door, down three carpeted steps. A low liquor table stood near the curtained window.

"You didn't tell me he was an eccentric." She had remained at the top of the steps.

"Who said he was an eccentric?" Godwin had a full assortment of liquor. "He just had an argument with his wife."

"Honestly, Mitchell. You can explain away anything." She descended the steps, her heels wobbling in the rugs. "At least he could stop and bring us inside."

"You don't understand anything. He doesn't want to bother us with his private affairs. And he's honoring us by not treating us like guests."

"All right, Mitchell. Forget it."

He had begun to mix their drinks, but now put down the bottle. "For Christ's sake, Tam, the man wants to finish mowing his lawn!"

She did not answer. Sitting now, her legs crossed, she was squinting into her purse. "You have a cigaret?"

"Here." He took the cigarets from his pocket and tossed them to her. They landed near her feet.

She picked them up. "Thank you." While he finished the drinks, she lit one. "Come on, Mitchell. I'm sorry. I don't want to argue with you all day. I'm sorry."

"Okay, but . . ." He stopped, not wanting to start it all again. "I mean, try to be a little tolerant." He put the drink into her hand, sat across from her. There was a dull childhood scar on one of her hard little knees.

"All right, Mitchell." She thrust her puckered lips toward him.

Leaning forward, he kissed her quickly, and retreated to his drink. "You like this house?"

She nodded, but was not listening.

"Come on, Tam, don't sulk on me." On the wall above her head was a long curved Japanese sword.

"I wasn't sulking. Honestly. I was thinking."

Mitchell sighed; she was quibbling about words. "What about?"

"I was just trying to figure out what's happened to us." She shook her glass, an ice-filled rattle.

"And what *has* happened to us?" He wished Godwin would come inside and rescue him.

"If you don't really want to know—why ask?" Her brown eyes were steady on him.

He rested his drink on the arm of his chair. "Because you'll tell me anyhow."

"I don't think you really love me anymore." She spoke softly, with no more feeling than if she had told him his shoelace was untied.

He shook his head, covered his eyes with his hand. "Oh, come on, will you?"

"You didn't let me finish." She hesitated. "You still like me well enough. But all the romance is gone, do you know what I mean? We're not in love like we were when we were dating. You're not making love to me and then going home and thinking how nice it would be to live with me. You don't have to win me. All the romance is gone out of it for you and you feel cheated."

For a moment, he could not answer. Surprisingly, she was right. He hid behind a question. "What about you, may I ask?"

"Oh, it goes for me too. I miss your being polite to me because you know you have to win me. I miss being chased." She sipped her drink. "The funny thing is: I don't mind staying married to you." She looked at him. "And I don't think you mind staying married to me."

She was right about that too. It would be too much trouble to divorce her—especially with no other prospects—and remarry, just to have the same thing happen again. But he did not say this aloud. Instead he stood up. "I have to go to the bathroom."

She smiled at him. "So do I. Tell me where it is when you get back. And don't worry. We're just like everybody else now."

He looked in the kitchen, but finding nothing, returned to the front hall, from plastic tile to carpet, and climbed the stairs to the second floor. On the landing, he paused to look out of a window, down onto the front lawn, where Godwin still worked, three rows from the sidewalk.

All the doors on the second floor were closed. He had opened a closet, and a child's room, when he found Godwin's family—his wife, whose name, he remembered now, was Cindy, and two children—on the bed in what must have been the master bedroom. The room was neat, the bed under them made, the closet doors closed, the cushions on a small love seat rounded, dent-free. Cindy lay on her back, an attractive woman, short, blond, nicely built, her purple skirt bunched around plump thighs, flowered underpants looping one ankle, her eyes and mouth open. The children, a boy in a blue bathrobe and a little girl with pigtails, one tied with red, the other white ribbon, had been placed so that they seemed to be nestling, asleep, against their mother. Godwin had even wrapped Cindy's arms around them.

At first, Mitchell watched them from the door, but strangely excited and wanting to see more, he crept closer to the bed. Cindy's neck had been broken, he was sure. The children had probably been strangled; dark blue marks ringed their necks.

He waited until his heart grew quiet, then tried to decide exactly what he would do, how he would protect himself, how he would remain uninvolved. He hoped Godwin had not mentioned their visit to anyone at the office. He decided not to tell Tam; she might do something stupid, like flee, filling the quiet street with screams. In a few more minutes, they would start home. Whatever Godwin did after that was his own business.

After another look at Cindy's thighs, he continued to search for the bathroom. He would have to give Tam explicit directions so that she would not blunder into the bedroom. A few moments later, surrounded by pink tile and washing his hands, he heard the power mower stop.

6

He dried his hands quickly, but Godwin had reached the living room before him — was sitting deep in a soft chair, a drink in his small right hand. Tam was leaning toward him, her breasts almost touching her crossed knees, listening.

". . . so I just pushed the needle right on through." He glanced at Mitchell, but went on talking: "It's one of those things you'd only do in the middle of a war. A lot of crazy things were happening."

"Mitchell, you didn't tell me John wore an earring. How could you forget that?"

He shrugged, sitting so he could see them both. When Godwin was looking at Tam, his blue eyes tired and half-closed, Mitchell searched his face for signs—of anything. But Godwin might have been sitting in a business conference, neatly dressed, listening intently, talking easily. He had not changed, except that now work in the yard had made him sweat.

"So, Mitchell, you had a look around the house." He held Mitchell's eye, without guilt, or sadness, or even a threat. But he knew that Mitchell had found his family.

That interested Mitchell most, that Godwin knew, but did not care, was not afraid of his knowing. He realized he was not in danger. "It's a nice house, John, especially the way the bedrooms are laid out. A family could be very happy here."

"Yes, I guess it could." He stared into his drink, then bolted a mouthful. "I'm sorry you had to come today, with us scrapping and all." He smiled at them both and went on: "It's not quite the way we planned it, huh, Mitchell?"

Mitchell shook his head. Godwin seemed so calm, so harmless that curiosity was overcoming his desire to leave quickly, although he had no idea how he would use what he might learn, or even about what he was curious.

Godwin was explaining to Tam: "We were going to make you and Cindy take the kids for a ride so we could watch the ball game in peace."

Tam laughed, charmed. "Oh, I see, it was a plot." But suddenly she was quite serious. "Are we really so hard to be around, John?" She closed her eyes; when they opened, she was looking at Mitchell.

Godwin shook his head. "No, you aren't hard to be around, at least not the way I think you mean it." He laughed, a snort. "Come to think of it, you don't even understand why we do need you around. You think it's love or sex or something like that." He stood up then, drained his glass, and walked to the liquor table. "It's hard for us to have you around in the same way it's hard for a lunatic to have his attendant around. Does anyone want something?"

"I do, thank you. That's a terrible thing to say." Smiling, Tam slid to the edge of the sofa, her pink skirt tangling in itself so that Mitchell could see the darker nylon at the tops of her stockings. She set her glass on the low table and returned to the sofa. "If it isn't love or sex, what is it?" Looking at Mitchell, "I'd like to know."

Godwin brought her drink, sat down, and smiled at Mitchell. "So you two had a fight today too?"

"Yes, we did, John." Mitchell glanced at Tam, who did not seem embarrassed. "But I don't think it was as bad as yours."

"Oh, Mitchell." Tam sucked her tongue. "You can't compare the fights two different couples have. They're always about different things."

Godwin was silent for a moment. "You're wrong, Tam. It's always the same fight, for everybody. The thing that *is* different is how bad the fight is." He hesitated. "At least for us, here. What I mean, when I was in Asia, I didn't see men and women have the same kind of fights we have."

"I know that. But there women aren't really free . . ."

Godwin laughed. "And you think you are?" He leaned forward, so close that Mitchell's heart, remembering Cindy's open mouth, beat a little faster. "An Asian woman isn't asked to do anything she can't do." He smiled. "You have the hardest job in the world." He was pointing at her now, a finger that could break a neck jabbing the air in front of her nose. "You have to try your best to keep us from growing up."

She sat up, slightly angry. "Now you sound like Mitchell. Why do men always say that women keep them little boys? Why blame us?"

Godwin shook his head. "I don't blame you for anything. I sympathize with you. You're right to keep us little boys. I only blame you when you fail. Cindy failed. That's why we had a fight today."

Mitchell was interested. "What *did* you fight about?" He was not certain that he understood Godwin. Perhaps knowing why they had fought, would help him understand why Cindy was dead.

"I wanted her to move to San Diego."

Tam looked around the room, at the soft chairs, the rugs, the tables of dark, deeply grained wood, and the paintings of children with large, black eyes. "But why?"

"Mitchell knows. Don't you." Godwin lifted his glass, toasting him.

For some reason he was getting nervous. "He's . . . he's been called into the Marine Corps." He covered his eyes, as if the headache gathering itself in his head might be eased by darkness.

"Well?"

"And I wanted her to move to the West Coast so that when I got a leave, I wouldn't have to travel so far to see her. But she wanted to stay here. She had friends here, she said, and she'd be lonely out there, making new friends and all, and the kids . . . they were sitting right there with us, eating breakfast, you know. They saw the whole thing. A fight like that, that's a bad memory, you can never be happy after you see your parents fight like that. You understand, Mitchell? It was a bad fight. An awful fight." He shook his head. "I . . . I hit her and the kids saw the whole thing. You see what I mean, Mitchell? So I made them go with their mother. Isn't that what you would've done, Mitchell?"

Mitchell thought it would be easy to say, No, but he could see the children sitting over their cereal, or cold scrambled eggs, watching. If it were anything like his fights with Tam, it would have begun quietly, a word, or a sentence studded here and there in the breakfast clatter. Cindy would be moving all the time, to the stove for more coffee, to the toaster, to the cupboard for sugar and jam. Godwin would remain at the table, asking a question, waiting for her answer, its sentimentality and lack of reason angering, disgusting him, until finally, when she was within range, he would let his hand speak for him, and, his training forever in mind, would see nothing but the column of white skin, small bones and muscle exposed between her chin and the top button of her sweater. His children would be looking at him, and he would know that his duty to them was to stop their minds, their memories. But still, Mitchell could not allow himself to be definite about such a thing, and answered: "I guess so, John."

"So she left you." Tam was staring at her hands. "Oh, John, I'm sorry."

Godwin nodded, smiled at her. "You see, she shouldn't have argued with me. She could've gotten what she wanted, in all kinds of roundabout ways. But she tried to be honest with me. That's what I understand now. It's like when a kid wants something you don't want him to have, you fool him. You give him something else and tell him it's a surprise, or it's special. But you don't argue with him. You don't go down to his level. And a woman can't fight a man on his terms or she'll lose everything. That's why it's so hard for a woman. She can't let a man grow up, because then terrible, terrible things will happen." He tilted back his head, emptied his glass, and tears ran across his cheeks and spotted his white collar. "Terrible things."

Mitchell looked at Tam, and found her motioning toward the door. He did not understand until she stood up. "May I use your ladies' room, John?"

Mitchell got up quickly. "You can go on the way home."

"You know we can't leave now, Mitchell." She stopped in front of Godwin, touched his shoulder. "When I come back, John, I'll fix some dinner and we'll stay until you feel a little better."

"But, Tam, I said we have to go." Mitchell tried again.

Godwin stared at him for a long moment, then turned to Tam. "It's the second door on the right."

"But, John, that's the—" He stopped, realizing she would find out now, no matter what he said or did. "The second door on the right."

Godwin waited until her heels disappeared into the hall ceiling, then leaned toward Mitchell. "You agreed with me about the kids, didn't you?"

"Well, I didn't actually . . ." He couldn't continue.

"It'll be all right. You have it made now." Godwin smiled. "You're safe."

Tam did not scream. She came down the stairs slowly, and for a moment, stood in the doorway, a little pale, staring first at him and then Godwin. Then she walked to Mitchell, slapped him hard, and stepped back, waiting to see what he would do. A monster inside him wanted to tear at her, but his fear of it was greater than the cold pain across his cheek. He held the monster until the pain was gone.

"Good night, John." She bent down and kissed Godwin's lips. "Call the police."

Godwin nodded.

"Say good-bye, Mitchell."

He thought it best to do as he was told.

7

Under a fist-sized sun, the road was clear. He drove slowly, to the right, away from the fence, streaked with the paint of cars that had gotten too close, which separated the two sides of the highway. Tam had not spoken since they left Godwin's house. She had put on her sunglasses, large green ovals with black frames.

"Tam?" She did not answer, did not move. Inside the pink skirt, her legs were crossed and once again, he could see the dark part of her stocking, and even the plastic button and silver loop that held it up. "Listen, the reason I didn't tell you what I'd seen upstairs was that I didn't want to scare you." She had opened her purse, shook a cigaret from the pack he had thrown her, and pressed in the lighter. "He seemed calm enough. You know what I mean? Besides, in a crime of passion like that, a man's not apt to kill again. Tam?"

The lighter snapped out and she lifted it to her cigaret. Her words came in smoke. "Do you think he raped her?"

"Are you all right, Tam?" The highway was not straight and he wished he could take a good look at her.

He saw her nod. "Do you think he raped her, Mitchell?" He was waiting for tears to flow into her voice, but it remained dry, though now she spoke more deliberately.

"When?" He thought. "I mean, he probably . . . hit her in the kitchen. When would he get a chance . . ." He did not finish, the answer coming to him.

"Do you think after he killed the children, he carried her upstairs and put her on their bed and pushed up her skirt and pulled down her panties and raped her?" She took a drag on her cigaret, held, then blew smoke into the space above the dashboard.

"No, Tam." He shook his head. "God, that would be crazy."

"I know." Her voice was soft. "Do you think he did that?" She shifted in her seat and faced him from behind the green ovals. "Put yourself in his place, Mitchell. I know you can do it. If you killed me, would you do that?" She smiled. "Would you want me that much?"

"Come on, Tam. You shouldn't even joke like that." They

rounded a curve and for an instant her glasses filled with sun.

"You understand why he killed the children. I'd like to know if you'd do that to me."

He laughed. "You see? You always get the wrong idea. Sure, I can understand his reasons, but that doesn't mean I'd do the same thing." The air conditioner did not seem to be filtering off her cigaret's smoke; he felt his stomach beginning to fill with it. "Besides, he probably didn't want to kill her. It was just what they taught him in the Marine Corps. I mean, he forgot his strength. If I ever hit you, I probably wouldn't even hurt you."

"Maybe so." She shifted again, and somehow her knee was touching the soft part of his thigh. "Of course, John's a special case. But suppose you did happen to kill me—with a paperweight or something— would you go on with it? Would you maybe feel my breast to see if my heart was beating and then get excited, looking at me with my eyes closed and peaceful, and carry me into our bedroom and slide down my panties and make love to me?"

"But I wouldn't kill you! I wouldn't even hit you!" He took a deep breath. "I mean, when you slapped me today, I wanted to hit you, but I didn't."

He felt her fingernails on the ends of the hair in his beard. "Oh, I know that, Mitchell. I could see it all on your face. You were very sweet." She slid closer, put her arm around his neck, rested her head on his shoulder. "But when you get worked up enough to hit someone, it's only because you love her. You couldn't get that worked up about someone you didn't love. That's why I can understand John doing something like that." She paused. "Can't you? I mean, you don't get worked up because you want to hurt someone, but because you love her and want her to agree with you, and just because she happens to die, you don't stop loving her and wanting to make love to her." She kissed the corner of his mouth. "Isn't that so?"

"Sure. But—"

She sat up so suddenly that he did not go on. "Take this exit."

"What?" He had not even seen the sign; she could almost have been looking for it.

"Take this exit."

He held the car to the curve, came out onto a wide cobblestone street, and went through a dark tunnel which ran under the highway. After a block, she made him drive into the black asphalt parking lot of a new, two-story motel. She told him she had seen it from the highway.

As they crossed the lot, its white lines bright as chrome, she put her arm around his waist, hugged him to her. "I haven't been treating you very well." She stood on tiptoe, kissed his cheek. "I wouldn't want to end up like Cindy Godwin." She smiled when he looked down at her.

While he registered, already wanting her, she stood beside him, a new bride, smiling gently. In bed, she promised she would always take care of him.

Then she allowed him to unleash his monster.

With the help of one of Tam's girlfriends, Mitchell had arranged a surprise birthday party for her. Now all the guests had gone home. He lay on his back, in his underwear, an exhausted basketball player in a white uniform. "You know how I got so drunk?"

"How?" Tam was in the bathroom, he hoped undressing.

He began to laugh. "There were twenty-five people here. Everytime I mixed one of them a drink, I mixed one for myself."

"I was watching." She came out of the bathroom. He could see her underpants through her nightgown. She slid under the covers. "You better get in bed. It's not the weekend, you know."

"I know, I know." He sat up, swayed, then lunged to his feet, and halfway across the room. She had the sheet pulled up to her chin. He made his way around to her side of the bed, sat down. "Did you have a nice time at your party? I wanted you to have a nice time."

She nodded, her hair bunching up under her head on the pillow. "I had a nice time."

He kissed her. "Well, you know one good turn deserves another."

"But brush your teeth first."

"Okay." He stood up, lurched toward the bathroom. Behind him, she was getting out of bed.

"Don't run away." He propped himself in the doorway. "Where're you going?"

"To make a phone call."

"It won't take long, will it?"

She shook her head. "I just have to make a date for tomorrow."

"Right now?"

"Especially right now. I won't sleep well unless I know it's definite." She started to leave the bedroom.

"Why don't you call from in here?"

She turned back, blinking. "Maybe I'm planning a surprise for you, Mitchell." She looked at an invisible watch on her wrist. "Go on. Your appointment's in five minutes."

He was laughing so hard that he squeezed hair oil onto his toothbrush . . .

OPAL

Rain began to spatter the windshield, just as Mitchell twisted off the motor. Very quickly the streets turned ugly. He leaned back, watching the drops slant in front of the streetlamp up the block. At least the rain had waited all that day. Most certainly, Opal had given Jake a nice outing in the park—the sun high but not warm in the near-white winter sky.

He reached for his briefcase. It was the type with two handles; twelve years old, one handle had pulled loose and disappeared. He opened the car door and slid out, dragging the briefcase after him—and watched his papers flutter onto the black, wet asphalt. Resting on his haunches, and sucking his tongue, he collected the papers, drying them on his sleeves. Then he walked the three blocks to his apartment building, hoping Opal's dinner was something he liked.

He entered the apartment through the kitchen's delivery entrance. Opal was feeding strained carrots to Jake, whose chin was orange.

"Does he really like that stuff? Hiya, Jake-boy. What kind of day did you have?" He removed his hat, held it in his hand.

"All right, didn't you, Jakie?" She scraped the carrot from his chin with a tiny spoon. "We had a nice walk in the sun. Didn't we, Jakie?" She tried to give him another mouthful, but most of it landed on his chest.

"He needs some false teeth." Mitchell stood behind her, looking down at the top of her head. Her black hair seemed soft, was parted in the middle.

"Don't you make fun of my boy here. He's doing all right." She wiped his chin with a napkin and offered him another spoonful.

"He doesn't really like that stuff, does he." Mitchell inspected his papers, estimating the damage. Five sheets had been completely drowned in the black gutter water. He hoped there were copies at the office.

Opal had answered him, but he had not been paying attention. "What?"

"I said he loves it. Don't you, Jakie? Love those carrots, don't you?"

Jake clamped his teeth, refused to open his mouth.

"Look at him, for Christ's sake. He hates the stuff. Don't you, Jake-boy?"

"I can't have you breaking down all the discipline I build up during the day." She smiled up at him. There was a black space between her two white middle top teeth.

Mitchell put his hat on a stool and began to rummage in the cabinets for a towel to dry the papers.

"What're you looking for?" She turned from Jake, a spoonful poised halfway to his open, waiting mouth. "Don't mess around in there."

"I'm looking for a dishtowel. I dropped these God-damn papers in the street. I want—"

"Give them here." She put down Jake's spoon, got up, and extended her hand to him. "Men don't know anything. Never try to wipe anything when it's wet. Wait until it's dry. Then you'll be able to shake off the mud. A little wrinkled, but you'll be able to read them."

"Where the hell do you pick up knowledge like that?"

"My job." She smiled. "I get hired to take care of you." She sat down and began to feed the baby, who was a year and a half. "Come on, Jakie, just a dab more." Under the white nylon dress Opal wore to work, her white bra cut into dark brown skin. He wished sometimes she would wear a cotton dress or at least a full slip.

Jake had clamped shut his mouth again.

"Look at that stuff. Carrots. They look like the stuff they fed my father when he had his coronary."

Opal turned on him, a mock scowl on her face. "If you can't help in here . . . Don't you think it's time you said hello to Mrs. Pierce?"

He nodded and pushed through the two-way door leading to the living room. From time to time, he wondered why he excused the way Opal talked to him. Not only did she work for him, but they were both in their thirties (Opal perhaps a year or two older), and he could not even say he was respecting an elder. When he thought about it, which was not often, he usually decided his indulgence of her had something to do with her taking care of his baby, cleaning his house, ironing his shirts, and cooking two of the three meals he ate each day.

The living room was empty. He went on through—Opal had put down a plastic sheet, which waited for mud, near the front door—and into the bedroom.

Tam was sitting on the bed, her feet up, bare, white, and small against the red spread. She was on the phone. ". . . it all fell out. I never went there again. If I hadn't been going away the next day, I'd have sued." She put her hand over the mouthpiece, gave him a hard look. "Hello." She puckered her lips and closed her eyes.

He bent to kiss her, but she broke out of it. "No. I'm telling the absolute truth. I have very fine hair. I get it set and then someone breathes too hard and it's all over my head . . ."

Mitchell removed his overcoat and hung it in the closet, noticing the mud on his sleeves. He wondered if Opal was right about mud being easier to take off when it was dry. It was a shame to see her getting fat. Colored people ate too much rice.

". . . pay twenty-five dollars and the next thing you know you're going bald . . ."

He loosened his tie, unbuttoned his collar. Then he took off his suit coat. He came out of the closet rolling up his sleeves and sat down in an easy chair facing the bed.

". . . absolutely right. Mitchell's here now and I have to get his dinner . . . Oh yes, Opal's still here . . . All right, I'll meet you at the gallery at ten . . . Good . . . That's good . . . All right . . . Good night, dear." She hung up, and stretched. Her breasts moved under her sweater. She was always saying they had sagged since Jake, but he could not see it. "You were late tonight." She produced a cigaret from a drawer in the bed table, and lit it.

"I got here the same time. I was watching Opal feed the baby." He thought of Jake resisting the carrots and smiled. "It must be tough being a kid and having to eat stuff like that. Looks terrible."

"You couldn't have been watching him all this time." She took a deep drag on the cigaret and blew smoke at the lighted end; it flared.

"No." He shrugged. "Opal helped me dry off some papers I dumped in the street."

Tam nodded. "You didn't even want to come say hello."

She took another drag—too deep—and started to cough, her breasts shaking.

Looking at her face, pink from coughing, he realized she had seen him staring at her breasts. Embarrassed, he retreated toward her and sat on the edge of the bed. "Sure I did, Tam." She was still coughing, her eyes staring at him through a film of water. He put his arms around her, hiding. Finally, when her breathing slowed, she allowed him to turn her face up, to suck the water from her eyes, and kiss her mouth. "Okay—what's the problem?"

She hesitated. "Jealous, I guess." She put down the cigaret.

"Of who, for God's sake? Opal?"

"No, not Opal." She was almost indignant. "I guess I feel guilty. Maybe I don't do enough around here." She pulled back and looked at him, waiting.

"Come on. We've got what everybody wants." He recited the list. "A nice place to live. A good maid. What do your buddies call her—a treasure? She does all the boring stuff and you have time to do the things you want to do, like go to the art gallery tomorrow."

"Still, maybe I should do more around here." For an instant, he had the silly feeling that she was testing him.

He did not speak for a moment. Since Opal had come to work for them (shortly after Jake was born), he had noticed that Tam seemed increasingly afraid of Jake. When she picked him up, she looked very like she was embracing twenty pounds of snake. She always seemed relieved after she had put him down. "Well, maybe you could spend more time with Jake."

She bristled. "Listen, if you don't think it's a full-time job telling Opal what to do and making sure"—she took a breath—"she doesn't steal anything, you're sadly mistaken." She pushed him away and leaned against the headboard. The cigaret she had been smoking smoldered in the ashtray. She took a last drag, mashed it out, splitting the flimsy paper, and lit another.

Mitchell was a little confused. "What's wrong with you anyway? You just said the same thing. And what's this business about Opal stealing?"

She went stiff, but spoke softly: "Don't you read the papers? People are so hard up for good help they'll hire anyone—even without references. And the anyones are robbing everybody blind."

"Oh, Jesus Christ!" He did not like shouting at her. "Opal had great references. And that doesn't have anything to do with you spending more time with Jake." He shrugged. "It wouldn't hurt for you to walk him instead of Opal."

"No, it wouldn't hurt." She hid her breasts behind folded arms; she did not want to and would not talk about it anymore.

"Okay." He got up and wandered into the living room. It was lit only by a small, wrought-iron chandelier, and looked as though no one had walked its floors or sat in its chairs for years.

In the kitchen, Jake was giggling. Mitchell pushed through the door and found Opal at the sink, rinsing Jake's bowl and spoon. Jake, nowhere in sight, giggled again and Mitchell located him under the table. Every now and then Opal would twist toward the table, aim with her index finger and make a popping sound with her tongue. Each time, Jake would giggle.

Mitchell sat down at the table and Jake began to play with his shoelaces. "What'd you fix for dinner?"

"I got you some nice veal tonight, and potatoes, peas, and apple pie. Some good veal. No veins." Drying her hands, she turned from the sink and smiled at him. She was wearing a pink half-slip under her nylon dress. A brown strip of stomach separated her white bra and the pink half-slip. "Come one, Jakie." She bent down and the dress stretched over her buttocks and thighs.

Jake crawled out from under the table and up into her arms. She stood up, the baby's hand inside the neck of her dress. "Time for bed, Jakie." She asked Mitchell the time.

He looked at his watch. "Almost seven."

"Oh my God, I got to hurry." She swung through the door, the baby in her arms, leaving Mitchell alone in the warm kitchen. He could smell spices, the cinnamon of the apple pie. The oven was cooling, clicking. He felt like resting his head on his arms, there at the table, and dozing.

He was still alone when the buzzer rang for the delivery entrance. He got up and opened the door.

The Black man was his height and very dark. He wore a pair of brown wool pants and a chartreuse bowling jacket with his name— Cooley—in gold thread over his heart. His eyes were red and tired. Mitchell stepped back, ready to slam the door. "Yes?"

"This where Opal Simmons work?"

"Yes, it is. What . . . ?"

The door behind Mitchell opened and he turned around.

"Hello, Cooley. I'll be right with you." Opal was slightly embarrassed. "Okay, Mr. Pierce, everything's ready now. Mrs. Pierce gave me an hour off so I could go out with Cooley here. I'll see you tomorrow." Opening the kitchen closet, she got out her coat, put it on, then picked up a large handbag, brown, surprisingly close to her own color. She took a step toward the door, where Cooley waited, jingling keys.

Mitchell found himself tasting vinegar; his eyes began to water. He paid her enough to expect better service than this, a decent report on how she had left the house, a respectful good-bye. And how dare she have such a person as this Cooley, in his outlandish bowling jacket, call for her at his house? Mitchell could not let her go without expressing his disapproval. "Just a minute, Opal. I want to talk to you. Tell your friend to wait outside."

Opal nodded. Cooley backed out, pulling the door behind him.

"Yes, sir?" She buttoned her coat, starting at the collar. Her brown hands moved down the row of black, shiny buttons.

He could not speak until her hands stopped. "Look, Opal, I don't want to hurt your feelings, but I'd be grateful if you didn't have your boyfriends coming to the door."

"I'm sorry, Mr. Pierce. This is the first time and—"

"Well, make sure it's the last, God damn it! Don't run your social life out of my house. You can meet your *men* on the corner. I don't want them hanging around."

"He just came. He wasn't hanging around, Mr. Pierce." She was being too submissive, almost as if she were willing to accept his insults to keep him from discovering a more serious crime.

"Listen! I don't want any God-damn excuses from you! Just don't have a whole lot of guys coming to my door!"

She lowered her head. "Yes, sir."

Now, very subtly, she was insulting him. She was very good at it; they all were—so good that he was not even sure what about her was insulting. That made him even more angry and before he was fully aware of what he was doing, he had pushed her to the floor, wrestled the brown handbag from her, dumped its contents on the kitchen table, and was searching amid hairpins, coins, lipsticks, and scraps of paper for the things he was certain now she had stolen from him.

WILLIAM MELVIN KELLEY

Mitchell was already in bed, but Tam was still packing the last case (small and square) with rattling bottles of perfume, deodorant, a tube of toothpaste, hair conditioner, and vitamin pills for the unborn child. She was only four months pregnant, but already her stomach stood out beyond her breasts.

"Why don't you save the rest for tomorrow?"

She did not answer, had turned her back, and gone to the dresser for her special suntan oil.

"Tam?"

"Maybe if I'm not finished we won't go."

"Sometimes I don't think you really want to go." He sat up. "It'll be good for you, relaxing, a little swimming."

She stopped and looked at him now, began to speak, decided against it, then finally: "Look, is it too late to call up there and tell him we only want the house for August?"

"Don't you want to go?"

"You want the truth? No."

"Why, for God's sake?"

"I just don't want to leave the city." She held out her hands, palms down, inspecting her nails. "This is the best summer I've had since I got here."

Mitchell tried to think why. As a matter of fact, because of a new situation at his office, he was spending very little time with her. "I know you want to stay with me, Tam. But you really need a vacation."

"From what?" She stared at him.

"Just the city." He paused, thought. "Are you worried about the baby?"

"Yes, that's it," she answered, it seemed, almost too quickly.

"But I spoke to your doctor. He said it would be good for you to get away."

"Then I'd better finish packing." She turned toward the bathroom. "With this stomach, I probably wouldn't be able to do very much anyway."

He fell asleep before she came to bed, and thought he dreamed that he heard her on the phone, wishing someone a happy summer . . .

THE SEARCH FOR LOVE

Tam made him stop in Truro to buy two pink-and-white donut-shaped life preservers. Without them, she insisted, it would be impossible to sun her back.

At Ballston Beach, she dropped one donut onto the sand, knelt before it, and into it inserted her unborn child. Using the second donut as a pillow she slowly settled onto the sand, lifting the top of her loose-fitting maternity swimsuit above her shoulder blades. Hers was the kind of skin that burned. At home that night she would have to sit at attention so the ladder-backed dining room chairs would not whip her. Still, she was determined to return to New York with a tan.

"Why don't you sit down, Mitchell?" It was more an order than a question. The life preserver looked like a fat halo under her head.

"I was thinking I'd run down the beach." He looked at himself. In recent years his navel had begun to sink into the flesh of his stomach.

"Sit down." She looked at him over her sunglasses. They were perched on an already blistered nose. "Before you give yourself a hernia."

There was a girl down the beach. Just as he and Tam arrived, she had run out of the water. She had taken off her bathing cap, shaken out her hair, dried her hands, and lit a cigaret. She was wearing the kind of bikini Mitchell had seen only in European movies. Now, like Tam, she was lying on her stomach, but without the aid of a preserver. She seemed quite tan already, though Mitchell had never before seen her on the beach.

"What are you looking for?" Tam spoke through the sunglasses now. They were not prescription glasses and she could see no more than ten feet in any direction.

"I thought I saw Linfoot down there."

"Linfoot never gets up before three." She rested her head on the donut. "You're crazy. Sit down."

Linfoot, a psychiatrist from New York, had rented the house next to theirs. He gave a party every night. Because Tam was pregnant they did not often go.

"All the same, I think I'll run down and have a look."

Before she could stop him, he jogged off.

Tam had made them sit halfway between the water and a high bluff covered with tough grass. Mitchell jogged down to where the sand was wet and firm; it was easier to run now. He was still watching the girl and as he got closer he realized she had untied the top of her bikini. Her breasts were flattened beneath her like small pillows.

He tried to think of something that would attract her attention, that would force her to lift her head, something that would impress her. He ran harder, hoping she would hear his footsteps through the hard-packed sand and look up. He called on his legs to give him all their speed, but the left one betrayed him and exploded. On his chest, he slid along the wet sand, a bomber without wheels.

"Hey, you all right?" She was looking at him now, her head raised, her nipples hovering just above the sand. His leg felt as if it had been torn off at the thigh. He could not even keep his mind on her nipples.

"Sure. Okay." He turned away, toward the sea, to hide the pain on his face. When she got up, investigated, and discovered how badly he was hurt she would think him brave. But a moment later, when he turned back, she was dozing.

He tried to get up, could not, and remained there, too ashamed to call for help.

Just when he was getting quite chilled, Tam waddled up, almost tripping over him. "What the hell are you doing down there? You scared me. I thought you were some dead animal."

"I think I tore a muscle in my thigh." His teeth were chattering and he found it difficult to speak.

"Oh, Mitchell, how'd you do that?" She was annoyed.

The girl had long since left the beach; she had not looked at him again.

"I was just seeing if I had any of the old speed left." The tide had been coming in; waves broke over his ankles.

Tam began to laugh, her stomach poked out and shaking. When all the laughter had left her, she helped him home.

WILLIAM MELVIN KELLEY

2

He spent most of September in bed. The first two weeks were the most boring of his life. He missed work; nothing interested him. In the morning Tam usually left the house. Soon after that, the new maid, a German woman, would take Jake for a walk in the park. That left Mitchell alone in the late-morning silence known only to housewives. He would try to read, but it was too tiring to hold up the books. He usually surrendered within the half-hour. He would doze and wake fully rested, unable to sleep again until after lunch. He would look at the ceiling.

Then he discovered daytime television. At first he watched the game shows, but they did not challenge or excite him. One day he pressed the remote-control channel switch in anger — and came upon Evansdale, New York, three hundred miles from New York City, on the Thruway.

He would sit in bed, a second cup of coffee warming his aching thigh, and wait for *Search for Love* to begin.

"This . . . is *Search for Love* . . ." a voice would tell him. Then an organ, with celeste attachment, would play the theme, filling the bedroom. "Brought to you by the makers of . . ." He would finish his coffee while the residents of Evansdale coped with heartbreak and tragedy.

He began watching in the middle of the breakup of Virginia (Ginny) Knickerbocker's marriage. Virginia was twenty-two. This was her second marriage. Her first had lasted only four weeks. As an act of teenage rebellion she had married a man who worked on the assembly line of her grandfather's textile factory. She had soon discovered that her husband was a fugitive from an insane asylum. He had tried to kill Ginny and, very easily, she had secured an annulment.

Her second marriage turned out no better, although this time her husband was sane. But he was fifty-seven years old. Ginny had married him in haste, causing the citizens of Evansdale to gossip. But they did not know that Ginny had just learned that she was adopted. Her second husband, the town doctor, whose daughter had died in an automobile accident three hours after her wedding, had understood when Ginny asked him for a divorce.

Actually, *Search for Love* was not primarily concerned with Virginia (Ginny) Knickerbocker (Reilly) (Spaulding). The main character was Virginia's stepmother, Nancy Knickerbocker, who was thirty-three—a year younger than Mitchell Pierce—and had once wanted to become a concert violinist. But Nancy's hand had been mangled (not noticeably) in an automobile accident and her ambitions had been mangled with it. She had returned to Evansdale and married Greg Knickerbocker, the editor of the Evansdale *Sentinel*, whose first wife had died of cancer.

A week after Mitchell joined the show, Greg hired a new secretary, Crystal Blair, a dark-haired girl from New York, who was fleeing her husband, a smalltime gangster. Soon Greg was coming home late and the Knickerbocker marriage began to limp.

(NANCY sits on the sofa, her hands knit in her lap. The living room is dark. Offscreen a door opens. There are footsteps. The door closes. GREG appears in the archway leading from the front hall.)

GREG: *You needn't have waited up, Nancy. It's well past midnight. (He comes to her and kisses the top of her head.) How's Ginny?*

NANCY: *She's all right. She went to her room directly after supper.*

GREG: *(He mixes himself a drink.) I had a very hard day. We didn't get the paper to bed until eleven-thirty.*

NANCY: *Greg, I've waited up because I want to talk to you.*

GREG: *I just told you, I'm very tired, Nancy. (He sips his drink and sits in an easy chair across from her.)*

NANCY: *We must talk tonight, Gregory.*

GREG: *You only call me Gregory when you're upset about something. (He sips his drink.) What's wrong, Nancy?*

NANCY: *(Tears glisten in her eyes.) You know very well what's wrong, Gregory.*

3

During the commercial, Tam returned from the beauty parlor. Her brown hair had been waved and lacquered. Compared to Nancy Knickerbocker's simple pageboy, Tam's hair looked stiff and wooden. "How's everything in Evansdale?" One morning, they had watched together.

He smiled, aware she was making fun of him. "All right." He had lost track of the time and wondered if there was one more scene.

"Ginny come to her senses yet?"

"Honestly, Tam, that happened two weeks ago. She got a divorce."

Tam walked into the closet; she could barely squeeze through the narrow door. "Is that so? That must've been something to see all right. Sorry I missed that." She backed out of the closet and sat in the easy chair. "Listen, Mitchell, we have to decide about Jake and nursery school."

"Yesss . . ." he started, but the organ music had already begun; there was one more scene. "Wait a minute, Tam." Nancy appeared.

"Mitchell, we have to decide. Enrollment closes this Friday."

"For next February?"

"Yes, and we—"

"Tam, please wait a minute." Nancy was talking, but he could not hear her. He leaned forward, though his leg hurt.

"Mitchell, I want you to listen to me!" As she spoke, she struggled to her feet, advanced on the television, and snapped it off.

Mitchell felt as if she had pulled out a fistful of his hair. He fell back into his pillows, his head and leg throbbing. "You could've waited."

She put her hands on her hips, slightly fat now despite a strict diet. "For God's sake, Mitchell!"

She was probably right. It was all nonsense. But something about the people of Evansdale, and especially Nancy Knickerbocker, had reached into him. They had more than their share of problems, but there was something simple and clean about their lives. A man might die violently, but he did not have to worry about wearing the correct tie, or who would notice it.

"Well? What'll we do about Jake?" She moved closer to him, threatening him with her stomach.

He looked at her from his sickbed and coughed once. "Perhaps it is time Jake got out and began to learn the ways of the world." The words came out hard and slow, like ball bearings too big for his throat.

"He's only going to nursery school, Mitchell." She laughed at him, turning away. "I'll call the woman."

"All right." He sank deeper into his pillows, and closed his eyes. "Do what you feel is best."

4

In another two weeks, Mitchell returned to work. The night before, lying next to the already sleeping Tam, he found himself wondering what would become of Nancy Knickerbocker. She could expect a bad time. Crystal Blair had turned the normally sensitive and level-headed Greg Knickerbocker into a love-crazed boor and Mitchell did not doubt that soon Greg would leave Nancy. There was no one in Evansdale to console her. Mitchell worried.

The next morning, he did not think about Evansdale. Late getting up, he rushed breakfast. The people at work seemed glad to have him back. On the desk in his office were two dark ties and seventeen greeting cards. He could not remember when the office had ever been so friendly.

He had worked two hours, catching up on correspondence, when his eyes began to itch, as if he had a grain of sand under each lid. He rubbed them until his secretary asked why his eyes were red. He paced his office, rubbing his eyes like a sleepy child, and decided finally to wash his face. Bending over the washbasin, his leg began to pain him, a hatpin through the muscle and bone. Then the bathroom musak began to play the theme from *Search for Love*.

He dried his hands quickly. Two floors above was a small room where executives sometimes watched baseball games. He could not even wait for the elevator; he chose to limp up the stairs. He was sweating as he closed the door and turned on the television.

"Oh, Greg, Greg, Greg." A white dot grew into Nancy Knickerbocker, who sat on the sofa, her hands knit into her lap. "Oh Greg, you don't know what you're doing. Crystal Blair has clouded your judgment."

"I won't hear you speak against Crystal. I've tried to be fair. I didn't plan for all this to happen. Don't you understand?"

"But it has, Greg. It has." Nancy looked at her hands. "It has happened and now you're asking me for a divorce."

Greg put down his glass on the coffee table. "I'm going now, Nancy."

"Going to her?"

"Yes, Nancy, going to her."

"I love you, Greg, and—"

"Don't say that, Nancy. It makes things no better."

"I love you, Greg, and I'm certain you still love me. I'll not give you a divorce."

"But you've got grounds . . . even in New York!"

"You mean . . . ?"

He nodded.

Nancy swallowed. "It makes no difference, Greg. I love you and I know you love me. You'll not get a divorce."

"You wait, Nancy. Just wait. When I'm through, you'll beg for a divorce." He glared down at her.

Nancy returned his look bravely, as the screen went blank.

Mitchell was still sweating, only now his palms most of all. He sat back in his chair and sighed.

"You don't really watch that stuff—do you, Pierce?" It was Naughton from Accounting. Mitchell had no idea how long the man had been standing just inside the door.

"No." He lied. "I'm watching to see if the show is suitable for one of our products." He left the room quickly.

Mitchell began to schedule his appointments so that he was always free from eleven to eleven-thirty. Five minutes before the hour, he would start the climb to the small television room, careful not to be seen. He always locked himself in now, leaving at the end of the half-hour, tired and upset. Greg was making Nancy's life miserable, badgering her for a divorce. Mitchell worried so much about her that his work suffered; he wrote the wrong letters to the wrong people. Mr. Cook was lenient, knowing Mitchell had been ill, but a threat was present in the man's voice whenever they spoke. Mitchell did not care, or rather cared a great deal that he did not care at all. Simply, *Search for Love* had become the most meaningful half-hour of his day. His morning built to it, and his evening began as its theme faded. The rest of the day held nothing for him — lunch, the office for three more hours, and then home to discussions about Jake's nursery school, or Tam's hair.

"You do like the way he did it, don't you?" She was standing in front of him, patting at her head.

"Sure, Tam." He looked at her, then away, trying to find something that would hold his eye. "But, why don't you wear it simpler, like . . ." he started to say—like Nancy's—but stopped himself. Tam did not know Nancy as well as he did, and besides, no woman liked being compared to another woman.

"Like what?" Her voice was insistent, slightly angry. "Like what? Like who, Mitchell?"

"Like in a pageboy, Tam." He tried to sound reasonable.

"I wore it in a pageboy when you met me and the first thing you did was ask me to change it."

Mitchell did not want to argue with her because he had nothing at stake, no point to defend. He stared at her, at her hair, solid and carved. "Okay."

"Don't okay me, buster." She started out of the room, stopped and came back, stood over him, her hands on her hips, as if she had just knocked him down and was waiting for him to get up. "And by the way, at this point I don't really care, but when are you planning to make love to me again? You better put in your order. Pretty soon the doctor'll cut you off."

The toes of his bedroom slippers were beginning to give way. He had bought them a size too small.

"What about it?"

"Please, Tam." He did not know what she wanted of him. "All right then. Come on. Take off your girdle."

"Thanks a lot. You're going to service me, like some mechanic. Give me a tune-up, check my oil and water, make sure I work all right. I told you I don't really care. I'm trying to keep my part of the bargain. But if that's your attitude. No thanks. I have better things to do."

"Why are you such a bitch, Tam?" He almost thought she might be able to answer.

But she did not answer. Instead, she removed her shoe, a suede loafer with a hard rubber heel, limped toward him, one leg shorter than the other now, and began to beat him on the shoulder. He listened to the smack of the rubber heel against flesh-covered bone, then very slowly got up and walked out of the apartment.

6

He hailed a taxi and went downtown. He did not tell the driver where, just downtown. The driver was a large man with a pink, creased neck—and a shrunken head hanging from his rearview mirror. It looked like the head of an hour-old baby, made of black rubber. Its eyes and mouth were sewn shut. Strangely enough, its hair was red. Mitchell asked the driver where he had purchased it.

"No place. Given to me."

Mitchell sat on the edge of the seat and rested his chin on his arms on the back of the front seat. "A joke?"

"No, for serious. In the South Pacific. It's real. Next light I'll unhook it. You can see for yourself."

They stopped at Ninth Avenue and Forty-second Street, a dismal corner. The driver unhooked the head—it had hung by its braided red hair—and thrust it into Mitchell's reluctant hands. They cradled the head as they would have a piece of dry ice. The skin was more like hard leather, rain-soaked shoes dried under a radiator. The mouth was sewn with wrapping twine. Mitchell wondered what he would find if he pried up the eyelids.

"Who gave it to you?"

"Head-hunters. We was mopping up Japs and took this small island, which they was living on. We was stuck with this bastard of a captain, who'd been on my ass and everybody else's too since Basic, right? So when we got to this island, he decided he'd start a little slave-labor force with the natives. So, anyway, we found a couple Japs on the island and had us a little skirmish there and in the middle of it, I discover my dear old captain right in front of me. So he was such a bastard I decided to put him out of his bastard misery, and lowered my sights a few inches to where his red hair stuck out from under his green helmet. After we wiped out the Japs we went around to pick up our dead, you know, as is only fitting, to give them a decent burial. But we couldn't find the captain's remains nowhere."

They had turned east, were crossing town now. As a lieutenant in an Asian war, Mitchell had tried never to antagonize any of his men.

"So anyway, just before we hopped to the next island, this delegation of head-hunters comes up to me and says a lot of mumbo jumbo and stuck this box in my hand. It was an old softball box, you know, sent out by the USO—they'd sent a ball and some gloves." The driver turned north. "I keep wondering if the head-hunters saw me do it. I look at that red hair and wonder. Wouldn't that be something if my old captain was riding with me all these years!"

Mitchell dropped the head onto the front seat. They had just passed the Automat, at Third Avenue and Forty-second Street, and sitting in the window, in a black sweater, had been Nancy Knickerbocker, eating what looked like a bowl of soup.

"Let me out here!" Mitchell opened the door of the moving cab.

"Hey! Wait until I pull over. You want me to get a ticket?"

They stopped at Forty-third Street and Mitchell ran the block, though his leg threatened him. She was still there, quiet over her soup, her pageboy covering her ears and cheeks, her eyes downcast. Mitchell wondered what she was doing in New York, three hundred miles from home.

7

Now that he was standing outside the restaurant, his nose pressed against the glass, he could not decide what to do. He knew Nancy Knickerbocker as well as he knew his wife, but since Nancy did not know him, he was afraid to walk up to her table, introduce himself, and tell her that if she needed anything at all, she could call on him. It was then too that he realized he was still wearing his bedroom slippers. Certainly he could not be wearing bedroom slippers for his first meeting with Nancy Knickerbocker. But he could not go home without knowing where she was staying in New York.

He entered the restaurant, bought a cup of coffee, and sat where he could keep her under surveillance. She was only three tables from him. It was strange to see her in color. He had always imagined her hair a dark blond; it was closer to platinum. Her lipstick was brighter than he would have thought; in fact, he had always been certain she did not use it. But these things were insignificant. She was as beautiful as ever.

Finally she stood up—shorter and thinner than television made her—and drowned her cigaret in the half-empty bowl of green soup. Mitchell waited until she had pushed through the revolving door before he followed. She walked north along Third Avenue, stopping now and then at store windows. Each time she did, Mitchell jumped into a doorway. He would stand there, waiting for her to go on, not daring to return the stares of the people who saw him lurking there in bedroom slippers.

After some blocks she turned east and walked to First Avenue, and entered an old six-story building with a new glass front. He waited protectively until she was safely inside the well-lit lobby, then started home.

Later that night, when he wrote her address in his small leather address book, he listed her as Nick so that if ever Tam saw it, she would not know who it was, or even that it was a woman.

8

Next morning, Nancy was not in Evansdale. Greg spent the entire night with Crystal, explaining to her that Nancy had gone to Buffalo to nurse her aunt. Mitchell knew better; Nancy was in New York, and he had to know why. Just before leaving the office, he called Tam and told her he had been delayed for a few hours.

"Do you have a girl, Mitchell?"

He sighed. "No, Tam."

"Then what're you doing tonight?"

"I told you. Some work to catch up on." He imagined her bulk taxing the tiny chair next to the phone table.

"Like what? You working for the CIA?"

"Please, Tam. I just want to stay here for a while."

"Don't whine, Mitchell. What time do you think you'll be home?"

"Late."

"Good." She hung up.

He left his office and walked to First Avenue, entering a bar across from where Nancy was staying—The Sons of Erin Tavern. It was an old bar with a large window onto the street. He sat near the window on a wobbly stool and waited for Nancy.

There were no women in The Sons of Erin; there was nothing soft or comfortable about the place. Everything was brown. The window was filmed with grease and soot. Mitchell traced an "N" on the window and squinted through the clean spot at her building. Then he turned back to the bar and ordered a bourbon and soda.

The bartender did not leave after serving the drink. "You been in here before?"

Mitchell wanted no conversations and tried to think of the answer most likely to cut this one short. "Yes."

Across the street, the lights in the lobby came on. Through the glass doors, the lobby seemed a stage set, waiting for actors.

"I thought so. You look like a Rafferty." He raised his eyebrows and rested his hands on the bar.

Some seconds later, Mitchell realized the bartender expected an answer. "No, no. I'm not a Rafferty. My name's . . . O'Connor."

"From the Jim O'Connors up at Seventieth?"

Perhaps he should have said he had never entered The Sons of Erin; perhaps it would have made no difference.

"No. I'm from Evansdale. That's upstate."

The bartender paid no attention. "Little Jim O'Connor—a lovely person, but a terrible disappointment in the casket. Cancer it was. He was a little guy at the start and after the Cancer let him go, he was down to fifty-seven pounds. He hadn't worn street clothes for a year and they had to pad out his blue serge to make him fit it. But then his head looked too small for the rest of him. Brien wandered in with a load on and didn't even know who'd died and they come over from Cork together. Hardly knew him myself—and I was sober."

"You talking about Little Jim?" A man in gray denim work clothes joined them; he had been standing in the shadows at the other end of the bar. "Little Jim. As strong as two elephants before the Cancer commenced to eat at him. But he had it easy, he did. Frank Foley really had it rough."

Mitchell wanted to move, but could not. He had to stay near the window. He gulped his drink and ordered another.

"Foley—what a giant he was! A big man, a full six and one-half feet tall he was, drove a trolley and then a bus. He was up in Harlem when a nigger tried to rob his money-changer. Stabbed him forty-eight times, the nigger did, but Foley hung on, saved his money-changer, and lingered on for the next year and six months until his great Irish heart give out on him. It wasn't just the stab holes; it was the complications. First his lung collapsed, then his bladder give up and he had to piss through a tube leading from his stomach to a bottle under his bed. Then because of that bad lung, his heart was working overtime and his feet begun to swell up. Finally he passed into the peaceful arms of the Virgin."

The bartender nodded. "Foley. A giant like you say. And Little Jim too. But I never seen anyone die as good as Neil-o Murphy."

"Neil-o Murphy. Yes . . ." The other man sighed. So did Mitchell. The bourbon was taking effect and he began to feel almost Irish himself.

"And it all started with his walking around barefoot."

"How d'you mean?" Mitchell could not help asking.

"Well, O'Connor, he was walking around barefoot in his own house, mind you, and he picked up a splinter. So you know Neil-o wasn't about to let no splinter slow him down. He forgets it. Two weeks later— bam!—his foot swoll up like a . . . But you think Neil-o would go to the doctor? No, sir, he lets it pass and then one day he faints away, right here on First Avenue and they take him over to the hospital and—you guessed it—gangrene! So they cut off his foot, but too late, and had to cut off the leg up to the knee, and then the knee itself. Then somehow it jumped over to the other leg and, well . . ." He shook his head. "Neil-o Murphy died in pieces. At the end, nothing was left but a head and torso. His coffin was only four feet long. You care to know the time between when he picked up that splinter and the day we each dropped one last rose into his grave?"

"Yes," Mitchell answered truthfully.

"Four years and nine months." The bartender shook his head as if even he found it an unbelievable length of time. "Jesus, Mary, and Joseph, could that man die!"

Mitchell agreed. "He certainly could!"

9

At ten o'clock, five hours later, they were still talking about their friends, dying or dead. Besides Mitchell and the bartender, nine other men stood at the end of the bar. "Once knew a snakebite victim. He was out hunting and one night a snake crawled into his boot. Try as he might, the undertaker couldn't ever cover up the black color the venom turned his face. It looked so bad that even his own sweet mother wouldn't kiss him. She just looked at him and shook her head. 'That nigger ain't none of mine!'"

Mitchell blinked the blackened cheeks from his mind and looked across the street for the two-hundredth time. The lobby was a hazy yellow square now, resisting the surrounding darkness. But he had no trouble seeing Nancy Knickerbocker on the sidewalk in front of the house. She was talking to a man.

Mitchell stood up, tottered, steadied and, through the greasy glass, watched them shouting at one another. He could not hear them, but their backs were bent stiff and they had begun to wave their arms. By now Mitchell recognized the man as Greg Knickerbocker.

"Snake poison ain't the worst. Spiders carry the worst poison. Why you ask? Because it's slower . . ."

Greg grabbed his wife's arms and began to shake her. Mitchell dropped ten dollars on the bar, pushed past the men, and staggered out to the curb. He had entered The Sons of Erin while the sun was still warming the autumn air. Now a brisk wind carried the couple's words across to him.

"You're nothing but a two-bit hooker. You know that? That's exactly what you are." Greg was still shaking her.

She seemed not at all afraid of him. "Eunuch! Let me go!"

Greg responded by pounding Nancy's nose with his right fist. A red splotch appeared on her face and spread downward.

Mitchell began to yell—a war whoop, and limped across the street. He would kill Greg Knickerbocker and end Nancy's misery for all time. He pounced on the man as soon as he reached the sidewalk, hands gripping at Greg's throat, fingers digging into the small soft spot at the base of Greg's neck. He rode Nancy's husband to the pavement.

Above him, Nancy was screaming, clutching at his hair, trying to drag him from her husband's back. Inwardly, Mitchell admired her; after all Greg had done to her, she could still submerge the desire for revenge; her compassion shone as brightly as ever. For an instant, he stopped mauling Greg to gaze up at her—the opportunity Greg needed; he rolled away, scrambled to his feet, and without looking back, disappeared around the corner, heading east.

Mitchell brushed himself off, concerned now about Nancy's nose. She must have thought him strange, because she began to back toward the door of her building. Or perhaps Greg had returned. Mitchell looked around; the block was empty. "He's gone now." He shook his head. "Don't worry."

"You're a maniac." She stared at him. "Do you know you're crazy?"

Mitchell was bewildered. Then he realized that Nancy had no idea who he was. His flying out of the night to rescue her must have surprised her. He would have to calm her or lose her forever. Her first impression of him must be a good one.

He smiled his very best smile, then transformed it to infinite concern. "I think you should see a doctor for your nose." The blood dripped from her face onto the triangle of silkish white blouse showing at the neck of her trench coat. "Do you have a doctor in the city?"

She put her hand to her face, and, as if for the first time, realized she was bleeding. She began to cry, half-hurt, half-angry. "That bastard would hit me where it shows!"

Mitchell was surprised to hear Nancy curse, but supposed she had cause. "Do you have a doctor in New York?" Her physician in Evansdale was Doctor Spaulding, Ginny's second ex-husband.

"Sure. Sure."

"What's his address? We'll take a taxi."

Again she looked at him strangely, her expression hard to see behind the blood. Then she sighed, shrugged, and gave him an address in Greenwich Village. "What the hell! I began giving it away a long time ago."

10

It was difficult for them to stop a taxi until Mitchell gave her a handkerchief to wipe the blood from her face. Her nose was red and swollen. Her lips were puffy. "Where did you come from anyway?" They were headed downtown now.

"From The Sons of Erin Tavern." And when she looked puzzled: "It's a bar across from where you're staying."

She nodded. "So, you're drunk?"

"No. I'm a fan of yours." How could anyone not admire her, he thought, after witnessing what she had endured and the spirit with which she had endured it.

"You really watch?" She was testing her nose the way a person does fruit, wincing from time to time.

"I know what you're going through, yes."

"Mister, you have no idea! Everytime I say something, he moves, or fidgets, or picks lint off his clothes. What an absolute bastard he is!"

Mitchell could not understand why she complained about such trivial things when her other problems seemed so much more painful. But then, Tam did small things that he could not stand—forgetting to put a new roll on the spindle when she used the last of the toilet paper, leaving him stranded in the bathroom. He supposed that such things entered into the charge of mental cruelty when the time came to get a divorce. Even so, Greg Knickerbocker was first and foremost an adulterer.

Nancy's New York doctor lived in a loft over a bar on lower Broadway. Painters lived in the other lofts. As they climbed a long dirty staircase—his injured leg was beginning to get sore—Mitchell smelled turpentine. The staircase walls were covered with posters and announcements for art shows. The topmost landing, unlike the others, was clean and neatly swept. Painted directly onto the orange door, in six-inch white letters, was the doctor's name: MENDELBLUM. Nancy knocked.

"You sure this man is good?" Mitchell whispered, looking at the name.

"One of the best."

"Who?" A woman's voice came from inside.

"It's me, Elsie."

"Winky!" The voice named Elsie began to struggle with the door's many locks and bars. "Winky!" Elsie herself was short, gray-haired, wearing round steel glasses, a pair of striped railroad engineer's coveralls, and a woven Mexican serape. She carried a paint brush. She stepped onto the landing, gave Nancy a hug, calling over her shoulder. "Marcus, it's Winky!" She smiled at Mitchell. "Who's this?"

For an instant, Nancy looked puzzled, but recovered quickly. "A friend of mine, Elsie."

Mitchell introduced himself. Elsie took his hand, and Nancy's waist and pulled them into the loft.

"Marcus? Did you hear me?" She shouted upward, sending her voice over the partitions which broke the loft into rooms. The ceiling was at least sixteen feet high; the light did not reach it. Her voice died in the high darkness.

"All right, Elsie. I'm putting my pants on, if you please." It was impossible to tell where the doctor was. His voice fell to them from the ceiling.

"Come on, Winky, sit down." Elsie led them into the living room area of a huge room. Twenty feet away was the corner where the old woman had been working—on a large canvas with naked boys running through what looked like a deserted city. Against his will, Mitchell was moved by the painting. He looked down at himself to make certain he was still covered.

Elsie rested her brush on a mosaic coffee table and knit her paint-stained fingers. "How's everything going with you, Winky?" Only then did she realize that Nancy's nose was twice its normal size; with her hand over her mouth, she asked what had happened.

"I got in a fight."

"Oh, Winky-dear." The old woman sucked her tongue.

"Why's she here?" Dr. Marcus Mendelblum followed his voice into the light. He was tall, mustachioed, and wore a pair of old-man's-gray pants with brown suspenders.

"She was in a fight, Marcus."

"So what's new?" He squinted at Nancy, at Mitchell, and back at Nancy. "Let me look at your nose, Missus Knockerbocker." Mitchell did not like the deep sarcasm in the doctor's voice.

Nancy tilted her face up toward the doctor and the light. He took the nose in his fingers, inspecting it from the left side and then the right, making faces.

"Not broken. But your fans'll be disappointed for a few days. So, did he do it?" He pointed at Mitchell.

Nancy shook her head. "In fact, he rescued me."

"Is that so?" He glanced at Mitchell, his disbelief as real as his mustache, then fixed Nancy in a sad gaze. "When will you ever learn, Winky? Your mother—God rest her—would die if she knew how you're living. Such men!" He looked at Mitchell again. "Six months ago you came in here with a broken arm; now it's this . . . gentleman . . . and this nose. When will you give up this life?" He shook his head.

Nancy stood up. "Thanks for the medical attention, doctor. It was nice seeing you, Elsie. You showing soon?" She had reached the front door before Mitchell realized it was time to go. He got up quickly.

"In a few months, Winky. Hope you'll come."

"Of course I will." Nancy's hands were working on the locks. When she had opened the door, she bent and kissed the old woman. The doctor was still standing in the living room.

When once again they were seated in a taxi, Mitchell discovered he had deeply resented the doctor. "Why do they always think they can meddle in your life?"

"They—who?" Nancy snapped.

"Doctors." He was not certain he meant that.

"Oh." She shook her head. "I don't know about doctors. But fathers always think they can, I guess." Before he could comment, she went on, her soft voice filling the back of the taxi. "You're coming home to screw me, aren't you? That's what you want, isn't it?"

11

He held the glass door for her, then followed her to the elevator. For an instant, he imagined how they might look from across the street, through the window of The Sons of Erin Tavern. He wondered if anyone seeing them would know that Nancy was the daughter of a Jewish doctor. Riding uptown in the taxi, he had tried to discover his exact feelings on the subject. She had not seemed to change, although her father's Jewishness might explain why every so often she acted strangely. At any rate, he decided, his love for her was not so rigid that it could not withstand even such drastic adjustments.

The elevator was a long time coming, but they did not speak. He was staring at Nancy, still surprised that his most cherished dream was coming true. Nancy did not often look at him. When she did, she would shake her head. She too seemed overcome with disbelief.

The apartment she was borrowing was really one large room. Off one end, there was an alcove which hid a stove, sink, and refrigerator. Clothes he had seen her wearing before, in Evansdale, were draped over the few pieces of furniture. She offered him a seat on a brown sofa. "I want to look at my nose." She locked herself in the bathroom.

Mitchell got up and inspected the room. There was a window above the kitchen sink, but it looked only into another apartment. As he watched, lights in the opposite window came on, like a movie screen, and, through filmy curtains, he was looking into a bedroom. A man and woman began to undress, facing each other across a large bed. When they were naked, the man, large and hair-covered, knelt on the bed, his head buried in the pillows, his buttocks high in the air. The woman went to the dresser, opened a small box, took out a long string of dark beads, crossed herself, and began to whip the man with the beads. A shining ornament hung from the beads, but Mitchell could not see well enough through the curtains to know what it was. When they began to make love, Mitchell turned away from the window.

When Nancy came out of the bathroom, she looked as if she had been crying. Mitchell rushed to comfort her, but she did not want him to touch her. She backed away and sat on the sofa.

WILLIAM MELVIN KELLEY

"Is there anything I can do?" He rested tentatively beside her. She shook her head. "Just what do you think you can do, huh?"

He had an answer for her. "I know some people. I can help get you a divorce." He put his hand on her arm, but her eyes spit on it and he took it away.

"I don't need a divorce." She kicked off her shoes, sighed, and stood up. "Okay, let's go. You have to get up. This is a convertible sofa and I have to pull it out."

He skittered to a chair, a bit confused. "Why don't you need a divorce?"

"Will you cut that out?" She removed and stacked the cushions on the floor, and opened the bed. Then she unbuttoned and unzipped her skirt, let it fall to the floor. Her slip was black. She turned her back, presenting him with a row of buttons. "Help with those."

He reached out and fingered the buttons, but then pulled his hands back. Even though he knew her blouse front was covered with blood, the back was blinding white.

"What's wrong?"

"My hands are dirty."

"For God's sake!" She turned, grabbing the blouse under her breasts, and pulled, sending buttons clattering across the floor. She unhooked her bra and slid off her underpants and half-slip.

Even when he had dreamed of making love to her, he had never imagined a nude Nancy Knickerbocker. He had seen everything else clearly. The room was large with pink cloth wallpaper and large, stuffed pink chairs and sofas. The ceiling was low enough to touch and quilted pink. The bed was almost as large as the room itself. The weight of many thick blankets pressed them together. But never had he seen Nancy. And now, here she was, her body white, and soft. She straightened up, looming larger in the room, feeding on it, absorbing the air until he could not quite breathe. "I have to wash my hands." He backed away, crashing into the half-open bathroom door; it banged against the tub. He closed and locked the door and took a deep breath.

"Hey!" Her voice was muffled, but shrill through the door. "Hey! What's the matter with you?"

He sat on the hard edge of the tub, at first only relieved, then gaining courage. It was as if he drew strength from the tile walls, the porcelain sink, toilet and tub, the brass faucets. In any house, the bathroom was his favorite room, neat, functional, hard, and private. He gripped the edge of the tub, as Nancy pounded on the door. "Is anything wrong? You're not slashing your wrists, are you? I couldn't go through that again. Please don't kill yourself in my john."

"Don't be silly. Why would I do that? I'll be right out." He was not yet ready to return to her, but did not know why. It could not be only her nakedness. No man was afraid of a naked woman, except perhaps a homosexual. Something else was wrong, strange. He got up, flushed the toilet, and washed his hands, watching his face in the mirror.

"Mitch? They call you Mitch, don't they?" No one had ever called him Mitch, but he liked it. "Don't you think it's time to come out?" Her voice had changed, was now patient and even. "I want to talk to you. Maybe you can really help me."

His face smiled. She had stopped pretending. She was being truthful with him and with herself. She had been acting before, bravely maintaining a mask—and only then did he realize it was the mask that had upset him. "I'm coming, dear. I'm coming now."

"I'm glad," she whispered through the door.

He dried his hands and went out to her. She backed away and sat on the bed, her eyes big, waiting.

"I really do want to help, you know." He smiled.

She nodded sadly. "I must need help all right." She looked up at him. "Aren't you getting undressed?"

"Sure." He began—folding his shirt neatly, straightening the creases in his pants, spreading his sweat-dampened socks across the tops of his shoes.

When he was finished, she opened her arms to him. "You silly boy. You really shouldn't be afraid of me. I'm not at all dangerous."

He knelt before her and kissed each white knee. "I know you too well to be afraid of you. It was someone else."

For an instant she did not seem to understand, but finally gave him her sweet, brave smile and pulled him up on top of her.

WILLIAM MELVIN KELLEY

12

Some hours later, as he was putting his clothes back on, he assured her that he would handle everything. He was acquainted with several fine lawyers who would defend her in court; he would call movers who would pick up her belongings in Evansdale; if she could not open charge accounts in New York he would vouch for her. All this left her nodding her head, speechless with gratitude. He kissed her astonished mouth, telling her he would return later in the day.

At home, he wanted a cup of coffee and went straight to the kitchen. After the fluorescent tubes had bubbled on, he found a saucepan and filled it with water.

Sitting at the table, waiting for the water to boil, he thought about Nancy, and made decisions. First he would tell Tam that he was leaving her. He did not doubt that he would miss Jake, but if he left before the new baby arrived, he would not be able to form an attachment to it. He could not miss someone he did not know. Tam's mother could visit to make sure Tam got to the hospital on time.

The water began to boil, sizzling up the sides. He found the instant coffee and reached for a cup. At the last moment, he took his eyes off his hand. Without his supervision, it knocked over a stack of saucers, which crashed to the floor.

He listened, hoping he had not awakened Tam. But a minute later, the bedroom door opened and his slippers came shuffling toward the kitchen.

Tam was wearing his bathrobe too; her own no longer fit over her stomach. Underneath her nightgown, Mitchell knew, her navel had been stretched wide and her stomach was as hard as a leather basketball. Her wooden hair had rearranged itself so that it was flat on one side, ballooned on the other. She stood just inside the door, her eyes closed. "Couldn't you pick some quieter way to tell me you were home?"

He was kneeling, collecting the broken saucers. He smiled at her joke, avoiding her eyes, hoping she would not ask where he had been. But she did.

"Would you like some coffee?" He carried the broken dishes to the garbage pail, spotless inside.

"What time is it, Mitchell?" She sat down at the table. His bathrobe fell away from swollen breasts and the hard stomach. He brought the coffee and sat across from her, thankful that her stomach was now hidden under the table.

"What time is it, I said?" Her eyes were half-open now.

"It's ten of five." So much had happened, he was surprised it was so early.

"Where were you? And don't expect me to believe you were working late—at least not at work." She began to empty the pockets of his bathrobe, of tissues, a comb, a book of matches. "You got a cigaret?"

He handed her his pack, careful not to touch her fingers. The match flame forced her eyes completely open. "Well? Go on."

He sipped his coffee and decided to tell her. "I was with the woman I love."

"Your mother? She's dead. Don't you remember?"

"No, Tamara, not my mother. You don't understand, do you?"

"Listen, Mitchell, you're hard enough to understand at five in the afternoon, let alone at five in the morning." She took a drag on her cigaret and stirred her coffee, spilling some onto the table.

For an instant, he wanted very much to hurt her. "I don't love you anymore. Do you understand that?" He leaned toward her, as if to push his words deep into her.

She nodded, knocking her spoon against the side of her cup. "Next question: who's your new girl, Mitchell?"

He had expected more than that. He was disappointed but did not give up. "I know you're shocked by all this."

"Shocked? Because you can't put your full weight on top of me anymore and run out into the street and get some poor, dumb girl to tolerate you. Come on, Mitchell, be serious. You probably paid." She was smiling at him, not a glimmer of a tear in her eyes.

"It's not like that at all. This is real."

She poked out her lips and nodded again. "Sure it is, Mitchell. But why don't you get some sleep, sober up, and then—then see if it's so real."

"That's why, Tam. That's exactly why. Your attitude. You think it's sex—something dirty like that. But sex is the least of it."

"Who is it, Mitchell? Anybody I know?"

He shook his head, lying. "Nobody you could possibly know. She's kind and patient and sweet and decent. Things you've never been."

Tam got up and stretched. "She sounds very nice. I hope you'll be . . . very . . . hap—" She could no longer contain her laughter. Her stomach and breasts shook in his face. "I'm going to bed. You working today or what?"

He drained his cup. "Yes."

"Coming home tonight? Because if not, I'll go visit somebody."

"I won't be coming home at all."

She yawned. "All right, Mitchell, have it your own way. I'll see you . . . when I see you." She pushed through the door, then poked her head back into the room. "Give my regards to your ladylove." She laughed all the way back to the bedroom.

13

He hated to admit it, but Tam had made him feel nervous and unsure. She knew him well—he did not like admitting that either—and if she sensed flaws in his love for Nancy, those flaws just might exist. When he realized this, he knew he would not be able to work, and that he would have to see Nancy as soon as possible after the sun rose. In the sunlight, he would learn the truth.

He sat in the kitchen alone until seven when the German woman arrived. One look at her chubby, pink face was enough to tell him she did not want him in her kitchen. He went into the living room, and remained there as long as he could, but he was in front of Nancy's before nine.

The building was different in the daytime. The sun in each front window blinded him and the lobby was dark, a theater in the morning. The superintendent had already mopped the hallway and elevator; the building smelled of ammonia.

Nancy opened only the peephole. It was the old-fashioned type, without one-way glass, and he could see her two eyes and a bit of her nose, which was still swollen. "What are you doing here?"

He responded with a smile. "It's Mitchell. You know, Mitch? I'm here because I love you. Is that reason enough?" He put his eye closer to the peephole. She was naked, her breasts creased where she had slept on rumpled sheets.

"I know it's Mitch. Go away, Mitch." She began to close the peephole, but he stopped it with two fingers.

"Hey, what are you doing?" She tried to return his fingers to him. "Come on, Mitch. Be a nice guy, will you? I have to get some sleep."

His fingers curled into her apartment. From Nancy's side they must have looked like a lizard's tongue. He leaned closer and whispered. "I just want to talk a minute. That's all. Then I'll go away and I won't come back." He smiled. "Until six, for dinner."

Through the peephole, her eyes blinked. "Look, Mitch, I really do have to sleep. I'll look bad enough with this nose. So . . ." She tried to pry his fingers loose.

WILLIAM MELVIN KELLEY

"All right, Nancy, I understand. But I have to tell you something very important."

She squinted, then sighed. "If I let you in for five minutes, will you please leave after five minutes? Because I can see myself standing here all morning."

"Sure. I know you have a lot to do." He placed his smile on view in front of the peephole, and, as an act of good faith, removed his fingers.

The lock clicked; the door swung open, and he stepped timidly into her room, seeing first the bed where, only a few hours before, they had made love. The phrase *the scene of the crime*, or rather the feeling of the phrase oozed through him. He turned to her, found her leaning against the door. He could almost feel the cold steel on her naked back.

"What's so important?"

He would have liked to sit next to her, to talk quietly for a while and then tell her all he had done. But he could see she was very tired. "I told my wife," he began, "that I love you and that I'm leaving her and that we're getting married as soon as you and Greg are divorced."

With each word her eyes grew steadily larger, until she no longer seemed to have eye sockets, just eyes. "What are you talking about anyway?"

He did not know what to answer; he was talking about so many things. He finally decided on one word: "Us. I'm talking about us, Nancy."

"Will you stop that? I hate that!"

"What?"

"That name, damn it!" She pushed away from the door and into the room—climbed into bed, pulling the sheet up to her shoulders. "Look, Mitch, I really don't think we should see each other anymore. It's been a pleasure knowing you, but you're taking it too seriously." She closed her eyes, then looked straight at him.

"But, Nancy, I—"

"Stop that!" She shouted at him, sitting up in bed, holding the sheet. "My name is not Nancy. Where'd you get that anyway?"

"Where?"

"Yes. Where?" She waved a hand at him. "Look, it's not important anymore. Call me . . . Nancy . . . if . . ." She stopped, staring at him with fresh eyes. "You think . . . oh, boy."

"I think what, Nanc—" He did not want to anger her again. "I think what, Winky?"

She continued to stare, her face softening. "You think that I love you." She dropped the sheet and began to wring her hands. "And, oh Mitch, that's my fault. Come, dear sweet Mitch, and sit by me." She patted the bed.

He was confused but did as she asked.

"When I came to New York, lonely and afraid, you were the only person who was kind to me. And really, if things were as they should be, you and I would begin a life together. But, Mitch-dear, things in this life of ours are never as they should be." She looked at her twitching hands. "I'm returning to Greg."

Mitchell's breath left him. "But why?" he struggled out.

"Because I must. I've just received word that he's . . . he's . . ." A tear appeared in the outside corner of her left eye. She took a deep breath and went on. "He's all alone now, a broken man, and I'm catching the first plane to Buffalo. In less than two hours I'll be in Evansdale, by his side." She reached out and stroked his hand. "I shall always treasure the memory of your kindness to me." She leaned forward and kissed his cheek good-bye.

Waiting for the elevator, he tried to remember the soft touch of her lips on his face, but it was impossible. Some woman was filling the echoing hallway with shrill laughter.

14

The walls of the hospital room were not the usual white; they could have been a light green. The iron frame of the bed was chipped brown. One of the patient's legs was covered by the sheet; the other was suspended at a thirty-degree angle from his body. His face and head were heavily bandaged.

Mitchell did not know whether or not the patient was awake until the door began slowly to open and Nancy entered. Then through the layers of bandage, the patient sighed.

Seeing her, Mitchell sighed too. She wore the white silk blouse, somehow clean, and a dark, tight skirt. Her nose was no longer swollen. "Greg?" She stood close to the door, as if expecting to be chased away.

The bandaged head moved from side to side.

She stepped into the room. "I came as soon as I heard, Greg. How do you feel?"

He did not answer; the bandages muffled his sobs. "Go away, Nancy. Go back to Buffalo, or go to New York. Go anywhere, but leave Evansdale and start yourself a new life."

"Do you really want me to go? I mean—do you still want to marry Crystal Blair?" She stood now at the foot of his bed, grasping the iron railing with her white gloved hands.

"Didn't they tell you?" He shook his head. "Crystal's dead. She was driving. She'd picked me up and I'd just told her that I wasn't going to divorce you." He tried to sit up, excited. "That's the truth, Nancy. Really the truth. It was all over between Crystal and me."

"I know, dear. I know you never loved her."

"I don't think I ever did, not really, not in any deep and lasting way." He paused for a moment, as Nancy took a seat next to his bed. "I told her I wasn't going to leave you, that I couldn't live her kind of life. She became furious and began to drive faster, up and down those roads out near Lyma. We must've been going a hundred, and I tried to make her slow down, but she wouldn't. She opened the window and the wind was blowing through her raven-black hair. She turned to me and called me a coward. 'You don't know how to live, Greg,' she said. 'You don't know how to live because you don't know how to take what you want. You're a coward because you always, always, always ask.' Those were her last words. Headlights appeared out of the blackness . . . on our side of the road. And that's all I remember until I woke up here. Oh Nancy, will you ever forgive me? Can I ever make it up to you?"

Mitchell saw Nancy's hand creep across the sheet and into Greg's. "We'll see, dear. You can, if you try hard enough."

Mitchell left the room, knowing they would want privacy. Or perhaps he himself wanted privacy. He was glad the German woman and Tam were not at home. For a while, he thought about getting into bed, but finally decided against it; in bed, he would think about Nancy. No, he did not want privacy at all.

He showered, shaved, and put on fresh clothes. If he hurried, he could put in a full afternoon of work, the best thing for him.

The blanket on their bed was light green. Beneath it, Tam slept on her back, her stomach silhouetted against the window's square of dark sky. It reminded him of a magazine photograph he had once seen, of an Indian burial mound in the middle of the prairie.

He rolled over, away from her, and wondered if the new baby would come early. At seven and a half months, she was almost as large as she had been just before Jake was born.

"You awake, Mitchell?" She did not sound as if she had been sleeping.

"Yes."

"Why?" She waited, then asked another question. "Not doing anything nasty, are you?"

"No, Tam." He did not want to talk to her.

She was silent for a moment. "Whatever happened to that girl you wanted to leave me for?"

"I'm sorry, Tam."

"All right. But whatever happened to her?"

"She went back to her husband."

"So you had to limp home." The bed shifted; she must be on her side now. "You see, Mitchell, your mistake was that you spoke too soon." She was whispering. "You should have made sure of her, before you said anything to me." Her hands were moving up and down his back, from his shoulders to his waist. "You played your cards all wrong. For a while, you could've had us both." She pulled loose his pajama top, began to scratch his back with her fingernails.

After a while, he rolled to face her, to kiss her, but she pushed him away. "You can't now, Mitchell. You'll break my water."

"I'm sorry."

It was light before he finally got to sleep . . .

TWINS

1

"Twins?" All these long months Mitchell had imagined one baby, sexless, faceless even, coiled, waiting—tube, arms, and legs. Now he tried to picture two babies. But the four hands, four legs, and two heads would not separate. Mitchell's mind created a monster. "Why didn't you tell us she'd be having twins?"

"You're no special victim, Mr. Pierce." The doctor's beard was a Vandyke, a gray triangle that dripped to a point just between the wings of his bow tie. He squinted over the rim of his coffee cup, as if even he could not believe it. "I usually don't tell until the last month or so. But you really had plenty of warning." He lit a cigaret and exhaled, smoke clinging to his beard. "Have another cup of coffee. They won't be cleaned up yet."

"Plenty of warning?" Mitchell wondered if he could have forgotten such news.

"Certainly. I told Mrs. Pierce last month—six weeks ago." He rested on his elbows. "You see, there's more than enough worry connected with childbirth, even for a second-timer like Mrs. Pierce, so when I realized she'd be doing, as they say, double duty, I kept it from her until the last possible moment. That's my usual procedure." He stopped, then as an afterthought: "Of course, I do tell the . . . charity people right away. They have a great deal to prepare for. But then, they always seem to know anyway. Black magic." Suddenly, for no reason, he was stricken with a series of dry coughs.

"But our apartment is too small."

The doctor nodded, the beard-point stabbing downward into his chest. "Fraternal twins." He stared at Mitchell, his gray eyes fastening for a long moment on Mitchell's nose, then moving up to his hair. "Mrs. Pierce *is* darker," he mumbled into his cup.

Mitchell smoothed his dry hair. "What?"

"I was just . . . wondering . . ." He was watching Mitchell's nose again, almost as if he expected it to move.

"What?"

"You say Mrs. Pierce didn't tell you?"

Mitchell shook his head. He and Tam had very little to say to each other.

"That's it then. Perhaps somehow she sensed . . ." He turned toward the counter of the hospital's cafeteria. Mitchell did the same, his eyes sliding along the dull aluminum until they came to a nurse's plump buttocks. Her black neck and face grew out of her white collar. Her nurse's cap sat atop close-cropped crinkly hair. "Many Africans study here. Very eager, those people."

"Do you mean she knew it'd be twins before you told her?" Mitchell realized that his confusion must flow from the entirely new idea that he was the father of three, not two.

The doctor sighed; Mitchell looked at him.

"Mr. Pierce, I think I owe it to you, not as a doctor to a patient's husband, but as one man to another, to give you a little course in elementary genetics. Would you like another cup of coffee?" He stopped. "By the way, just where are you from?"

"Me? New York."

"Would you mind me asking how long your . . . people have been here?" The doctor squinted again, pained.

Mitchell was embarrassed; he did not like talking about his family. "Since 1664. My whatever-you-say was one of the three hundred men with Colonel Nicolls when he took New Amsterdam from the Dutch. But—"

"And your wiffffe?"

Mitchell did not like the way the doctor held onto the "f" in the word. "Washington, the city. What is all this?"

"That must be it. Mr. Pierce, I have to explain something to you, about your babies. But first I feel compelled to say that with conditions as they are today, this is a very understandable situation. It's a pity, I suppose, you must discover it under these circumstances. After all, the children are not really responsible. As I started to say, it's no more than a genetic accident. According to scientific theory, things like this aren't supposed to happen. But then," he shrugged, "we don't know everything."

Mitchell did not at all understand the doctor, but something terrible was lurking in the air between them. He leaned forward into that terrible thing. "Is something . . . wrong . . . with one of the babies?"

WILLIAM MELVIN KELLEY

The doctor hesitated. "No ... no ... not the way I think you mean it. They're both ... healthy. But one of them ... its appearance ..." He stopped to light another cigaret. "You understand, they are fraternal twins. That means—"

"That two eggs? Dropped into the ... the ..."

"That's right. Just the same as if your wife had two perfectly normal pregnancies, only at the same time."

"But one isn't normal. What's wrong with it?"

Two or three nurses looked at their table, toward his rising voice.

"As I say," the doctor whispered, "nothing is exactly wrong with it. In fact, if anything it's the healthier of the two. Tell me, Mr. Pierce, how much do you know about your wife's family?"

Mitchell's confusion was tiring him; he slumped into his chair. "About as much as the usual, I guess."

"Yes, well, these things can go all the way back to before the Civil War, though the chances are remote that it would show itself so alarmingly." A look of deep sympathy, even pity, came into the doctor's face. "You don't understand, do you, Mr. Pierce."

Mitchell shook his head.

The doctor looked at his watch. "We can go up now. I imagine that's the best way. Nothing I can say will make it any less difficult." He stood up. "Shall we go?"

Mitchell followed obediently.

2

The elevator ride was smooth, and silent; they did not speak. Stepping into the corridor, Mitchell noticed a group of nurses gathered before a large plate-glass window. Among them was the nurse who had taken Tam's suitcase when they arrived at the hospital early that morning. She did most of the talking now, while the others, some Black, some white, listened quietly. The nurse who lectured was white and the faces of the other white nurses seemed troubled. The Black girls, most of them standing on the outside of the group, were smiling. As Mitchell and the doctor got nearer the window, the lecturer saw them, and whispered to the others. They all scattered, disappearing into rooms and hallways, except for a Black nurse, who came toward Mitchell and stopped. "You have a lovely baby, Mr. Pierce."

Mitchell noticed the doctor turn away. The girl was gone before he could thank her.

The doctor reached out his hand. "Have you those cards I gave you, Mr. Pierce?"

Mitchell searched his pockets, found the cards, and handed them over. The doctor marched ahead of him. By the time Mitchell reached the glass, the doctor had stepped back. "They're already right in front." He seemed not to know what more to say. "I'm going to look in on your wife."

And he was gone.

Mitchell stepped up to the window. Four babies lay in white plastic baskets just inside the glass. The first, on the left, sleeping on its side, was Black, a film of gray over its brown skin, its curly hair matted to a lumpy head. Its nose seemed much too wide for its face, the nostrils large and round. The second from the left was bald. Its skin too was grayish, its nose half the size of a dime. On its left wrist was a tube of plastic: inside the tube, a strip of paper with Mitchell's name: PIERCE.

"It looks all right," he whispered to himself.

He inspected the third, bald also, with the same gray skin as the one he knew was his. He could not see its bracelet. But it was his; he knew because the fourth baby was much redder, must have been at least a week old, its straight black hair dry.

So numbers two and three were his. But he was puzzled; neither seemed at all deformed. There were no strange bumps; their limbs looked straight. He counted the fingers on the three hands he could see; one of number three's hands was hidden beneath the thin blanket. Perhaps the trouble was inside, no stomach, or two stomachs in one and none in the other. That happened sometimes. But the doctor, he remembered now, had mentioned something about its appearance.

He bent closer to the window and inspected them again, and noticed now that number three was a bit more pink than number two. That was it; either number two was too gray or number three was too red. But he could not decide which and wished the doctor would return.

"Hey, I want you to got a cigar. He from home; qué palabra? smug-led from Cuba." The Cuban, a large head and chest on short bowed legs, was slapping Mitchell's left shoulder. He was fair, with light eyes and straight, oily black hair. "You look at my son, hah? Wow, I got a big, beautiful son there."

"He's big, all right." Mitchell looked at the week-old. "How old is he?"

"Three hours already. He big." He began to pound his chest with his fist. "He big, right? Like me. I'm bull. Big chest, little legs. A bull."

Mitchell was truly impressed. "Three hours? He's big, all right." He took a step to his right to get a better look at the week-old. Perhaps at close range, he would be able to see signs of the battle of birth. He found none. The baby was indeed a bull. "Three hours? I wouldn't believe it if you weren't telling me."

"What you do?" The Cuban's voice was brittle with suspicion.

Mitchell straightened up and smiled. He had not meant to question the Cuban's honesty. He had heard that such people were very tender about these matters. "I only meant . . ." He stopped when he saw the puzzled look on the Cuban's face.

"What you do? You look at wrong baby. This one." He tapped the glass, leaving a fingerprint. "This one."

The Cuban pointed not at the week-old, but at one of Mitchell's new twins, number three.

"Oh. Well. I think . . . you must be mistaken."

"Me taken? Shit! What you say, hombre? Aquí, aquí. My son."

Mitchell shook his head slowly; he would continue to be reasonable. "If you could see the band on its wrist, you'd see it was mine."

"No, mine!" The Cuban snapped to attention, then quietly: "You crazy, man." For the next twenty seconds, it was all Spanish, very fast, not popping like Puerto Rican, but a little clearer with a whistling quality to it.

Mitchell reached out and tried to calm him, but the Cuban shook away his hand.

"You no touch me, crazy! Listen, I am here before about five minutes. Are cuatro niños here. Número uno: el negrito. Número dos: el blanco. Número tres: muchacho mio. Número quatro: el grande. You understand? Now, número cuatro, he is here when my son is come. Even I meet his father. Mr. . . . Mr. . . . Papaleo, an Italian? Bald? You see him? No, you don't see nothing. So, I go away five minutes, to the john, and when I come back, you are here and you are so in love with my son that you him want to steal." He squared his shoulders, which were quite broad. "I no let you, man. I no let you."

Mitchell had read about such situations, hospital mix-ups, courtroom battles, the fathers grim as winter; the mothers crying. And worse. He looked at the four babies, especially at number three and thought he saw now that not only was it red, but that it did not look anything like him or Tam.

He tapped, then pounded with his fist on the window, which began to quiver. Behind the glass, in their plastic baskets, the noise broke into the babies' sleep. The week-old, Papaleo, began to cry, arms and legs jerking like an unoiled mechanical doll. The Cuban's son—Mitchell knew now that it was not his own—began to rock from side to side. His baby wrinkled its face as if the sound of Mitchell's fist was an evil odor. Number one rolled from side to back, yawned, and for the first time, Mitchell could see the band on its wrist.

He stopped pounding.

El negrito, as the Cuban called it, was named Pierce.

3

But the knocking had already brought seven nurses, running, and the doctor. On the other side of the glass, two nurses, bandits in white masks, were snatching the babies away from the window. The remaining five nurses ringed Mitchell and the Cuban as if to pounce with straitjackets and hypodermic needles loaded with tranquilizer. The doctor hovered behind them; now and again his head would appear over the shoulder of one of the nurses. Mitchell backed up against the glass and waited.

"He's all right. He's all right." Mitchell could not see the doctor.

"But, doctor, he was trying to break the glass."

"No, no. He's all right. He's just had a shock." The doctor moved from nurse to nurse, an advocate. "He didn't know. You understand? He didn't know until just now. But," peering at Mitchell through a space between two nurses, "he's calm now. He's all right."

The nurses began to relax. The Cuban looked at the crazy North Americans.

"Are you all right now, Mr. Pierce?" The doctor called from behind the wall of nurses.

Mitchell nodded.

"You see, girls? He's all right now."

The nurses, after looking long and hard at the new fathers, began to disband. "We'll be close just in case."

"Two of them together and you have a riot," commented one of the white nurses.

Finally the corridor was empty except for the three men.

The doctor patted Mitchell's arm. "I'm truly sorry, Mr. Pierce." Mitchell did not know if the apology was for the nurses or the baby.

The Cuban's eyes jumped from one man to the other, back and forth. "He crazy—right, doctor?"

The doctor frowned. "Certainly not. And what exactly is your business in this hospital?"

"Me?" The Cuban came to attention. "To see my son. You see him? A bull. This crazy want to steal my son."

"I assure you, nothing was further from his mind."

"I not so sure." He turned and began to tap the glass, motioning to one of the nurses to push his son closer to the window. Then he rested his head on the glass, watching.

"Are you all right now, Mr. Pierce?" The doctor continued to stroke Mitchell's arm.

"Isn't there some mistake? I mean, that *is* the baby you . . ."

"Unfortunately. I was right there. In fact, it came first."

"But how?"

"Not to joke, but the usual way, I'm afraid." The doctor had been inspecting the polish on his shoes. "Do you recall the conversation we had in the cafeteria?"

Mitchell tried. All the doctor had really said was that Tam had given birth to twins. Then, Mitchell realized now, he had tried to tell him that one of the babies was . . . colored. He had now seen that for himself, but he could remember nothing else.

The doctor knew he did not understand. "The Civil War?" He raised his eyebrows. "Colonel Nicolls . . . Washington?"

Tam was from Washington. Tam had given birth to a . . . colored baby. Tam then, the doctor was thinking, must be . . . Mitchell began to laugh. "But that's impossible. I understand you now, but that's impossible. An ancestor of Tam's was with Major General Robert Ross when the British invaded Washington in 1814."

The doctor was not cheered by this information.

Mitchell stopped laughing. "But then how . . . ?" He thought. "Of course, neither of our families has ever been really wealthy." Finally, he shook his head. "No. It's impossible."

"Well," began the doctor, "there's only one other possibility." He hesitated. "Superfecundation. But, oh God, that may be worse."

"What? Super . . . ?"

"Superfecundation, Mr. Pierce. Very rare. Perhaps . . . you'd better just accept the situation as is."

"No." Mitchell went over it again and shook his head. "I mean, how can I? It can't really be any worse. Can it?"

The doctor was thinking. "In fact, superfecundation seems quite likely in this case. The child, after all, is quite dark."

"That what he got—huh, doctor? This super . . . thing?" The

WILLIAM MELVIN KELLEY

Cuban had turned from the glass.

The doctor looked at him, but did not answer. He took Mitchell's arm and pulled him away, across the corridor. The Cuban shrugged and returned to his son.

"As you know, Mr. Pierce, your wife has given birth to fraternal twins." Eight years before, Mitchell had arranged his mother's funeral. The doctor talked now as the funeral director had talked then. "This means that not one, but two eggs were present in your wife's womb." The doctor knit his fingers. "Superfecundation is the fertilization of those two eggs within a short period of time by sperm cells from two different intercourses. Now obviously, if you had fertilized both eggs, no one would be able to distinguish it from usual two-egg twinning. But if your wife had . . . relations with another man, who is very different physically from you, and each of you fertilized one egg, each of you would pass his traits on to the particular twin he had fathered. Do you understand, Mr. Pierce?"

Mitchell thought he did, but was afraid to admit it.

"Fantástico!" The Cuban turned from the window. "His wife she got two babies, but he is father of only one. Fantástico!"

Mitchell looked at the doctor, who nodded his head. "Unfortunately, that's the situation. Unless, of course, the deviate strain is in your wife's family background."

Mitchell shook his head.

"In that case, Mr. Pierce, your wife is an adulteress." The doctor seemed almost to want to hurt him. "And, may I say, not a very lucky one."

"Fantástico!"

4

The doctor told Mitchell that Tam was tired, groggy, and probably would make no sense until the next day. "Nothing will change before tomorrow, Mr. Pierce. Go home and get some rest. Face the new day with a clear mind, if at all possible."

Mitchell knew the doctor was right; he had seen Tam minutes after Jake had been born. She had looked at him, smiled with effort, and asked if he had seen the baby. Before he could answer, she had fallen asleep.

He took the elevator down to the street, hailed a taxi, and went home. Jake had been in Washington with Tam's mother for two weeks; the maid had left for the evening—the apartment was empty. Even before he removed his overcoat, he wandered from room to room, finally sitting on Jake's bed. It smelled of warm milk, and he had to force himself to remain there. Once, he had liked Jake very much. But the boy had become too delicate, a whiner. As he thought about Jake, he realized that the boy had begun to go bad almost eighteen months before, soon after Mitchell had fired Opal Simmons. She had been very good with Jake, good with all of them. But Opal had been a thief. Tam had insisted they never again hire a nigger, had picked a German woman.

He knew he had one thing to do—call Tam's mother—and he was not looking forward to it. He liked his mother-in-law, but whenever he talked to her, especially on the phone, his stomach always began to ache. Yet he could never discover what about her upset him. He decided that he would not tell her everything, just that Tam had given birth to twins, both healthy.

In his overcoat and scarf he sat down at the phone table and placed the call. "Hello . . . Mother?" He and Tam had been married five years, but he still hesitated over the word. "This is Mitchell."

"Hello, Mitchell. Is everything all right?"

"Fine." On the phone table was a small white pad. Page after page was filled with Tam's signature. Sometimes she had written Tam Pierce, sometimes her maiden name, and on one page just Tam J. or Tam Johnson, and a number. Mitchell tried to recall a Johnson that Tam knew, and finally decided it was the name and number of a small grocery store nearby. Strange that she imagined herself married to the short, parrot-nosed grocer.

"Well?"

"Tam had twins, Mother." He tried to sound happy, but knew he had failed.

"Of course. That's what she was supposed to have. Is anything wrong with them?"

"No." Under layers of cotton and wool, his stomach began to fill with gas.

"Don't lie to me, Mitchell. Tell me what's wrong with them." Her voice was very young. She sounded a great deal like Tam, except that she used no slang.

"Really, nothing's wrong. I'm just tired, I guess."

"New fathers are supposed to be tired."

He did not answer. He was looking at Tam's handwriting, the letters as wide as they were tall, the "i" dotted with a tiny circle. Her handwriting slanted slightly backward.

"Mitchell, what's wrong with you?"

"Nothing, Mother."

There was a long silence from Washington, then: "Jake is still up. He's eating a banana, but he might put it down long enough to talk to you. Say hello to your father, Jake."

Mitchell could hear banana breaking between small white teeth.

"Hello, Jake. You have a little brother and a little sister now . . ."

Jake breathed into his ear through miles of wire and a clogged nose.

"This is Daddy, Jake."

"Say hello, dear." There was a grunt, an empty silence, then a scream. Jake had begun to cry.

"What on earth did you say to him?"

"I didn't say anything." Mitchell shrugged, as though she could see him.

"You know, Mitchell, this child is in very poor condition. I really think he should stay with me at least two more weeks. I'll talk to Tam about it."

"All right, Mother."

"Good night, Mitchell." She hung up.

"Good night, Mother." Into the dead phone.

His stomach flaming, he took off his overcoat, exposing the heat to the air. He did not loosen his tie or remove his suit coat. Somehow he expected someone to visit—perhaps one of Tam's friends—and he wanted to look neat. Then he went into the kitchen to get something to eat.

He made himself a sandwich, sat down in the living room, even though Tam did not like him to eat there, and turned on the television set to watch the news. A war was showing. The reporter asked a wounded soldier if he was in pain. The boy had stepped onto a land mine and his right leg had disappeared. He took three drags on a cigaret, and then, surprising the reporter, and Mitchell too, he died. When the commercial began, Mitchell snapped off the set and went to bed.

5

Tam was sitting up, burying black needles in pink wool, when Mitchell entered her room the next afternoon. She looked at him, her fingers still working. "Hello, Mitchell. This is for one of the babies. You see them?"

All the way to the hospital, he had been hoping that he would find her sheepish, repentant. "Yes. I . . ."

"Aren't they beautiful?" She lifted the row of knots closer to her nose. "God damn, I made a mistake." She slid the needles out of the loops of yarn.

"Tam?" Mitchell ventured from just inside the door to the foot of her white, iron bed. "What about that baby?"

"Which one?" She was threading the needle back into the loops. "I had two, you know, Mitchell. Didn't you see them both?"

He looked at the top of her lowered head. She had not been to the hairdresser in some weeks. Her hair was slightly waved, covering all but the lobes of small pink pierced ears, ringless now. He could see the dark empty holes—spots. She was wearing a white hospital nightgown. "What did you do, Tam?"

"Now don't you think that's a silly question, Mitchell?" She smoothed a space for her knitting between her blanket-covered thighs, then began to nod her head too gravely. "Yes, yes, I know. You want to have a very, very serious talk. Go on."

He rested his hands on the smooth cold white railing. "Yes. Well, I really can't have this, Tam." Her eyes were smiling. "I understand that things haven't been going well with us. So I do understand . . ."

"Yes?" She was bored.

"Damn it, Tam, you have to give it away!" The words seemed almost to have created the idea.

"Which one, Mitchell? I had two." She smiled.

"Don't pretend, Tam. You know what I'm talking about." He gripped the railing, shaking the bed.

"Take it easy, Mitchell. I'm all stitched up."

He apologized.

But she continued: "It stings when I go to the bathroom. You should see these young little Rican girls. They're all fifteen years old. In to have a baby one day, the next day their stomachs are just as hard and flat. And they walk like nothing at all'd happened." She spoke with some small touch of admiration. "So, anyway, go on."

He looked at his shoes. "What I meant before about understanding how you felt?" His shoes needed a polish. "I know I haven't been a model husband either. It takes two to make a marriage."

"Sometimes. Look, Mitchell, what are you trying to say?"

"I want to know about that baby." He noticed an edge of whine in his voice, promised himself to sound more forceful.

"My baby. What do you want to know?" She closed her eyes for a moment.

"I want to know who the father is." He resisted an urge to stamp his foot.

She raised her eyebrows. "Why, you, of course."

"We both know I'm not the father of that baby. And neither of us have any colored blood in our families. The doctor explained it to me."

"You can't always tell." She paused. "But you're right. Cooley, I guess."

Mitchell did not understand.

"You don't remember Cooley. You should always remember the important people in your life, Mitchell." Suddenly, she sat up straight. "All right, Mitchell, stop joking. You don't remember Cooley?"

He shook his head.

"Do you remember Opal Simmons?"

He did. He had been disappointed when he discovered Opal was a thief. She had seemed so nice and quiet. Cooley. The night he fired her, had stopped her escape, knocked her down and searched her purse for his belongings, Opal had been just about to go on a date. A Black man had come to the delivery entrance and asked for her. "You mean Opal's Cooley? In the chartreuse jacket?"

"I mean my Cooley in the chartreuse jacket."

"Where is he now?"

She shrugged. "I really couldn't tell you. I saw him a couple of times after we got back from the Cape, when you were sick, but I haven't seen him for about six weeks—after the doctor cut us off."

"You were seeing him up to six weeks ago?"

"Was there any reason not to?"

He shook his head slowly. "What are we going to do, Tam?"

"You mean, what are you going to do?"

He looked at his hands resting lightly on the white iron railing, watched them curl into fists and jump to his sides. Tam's face was very pale, a great distance away from him across the white blanket. He began to beat the bones of his hips and thighs. "How can you be this way to me? How can you? I've made some mistakes, but I don't deserve this!"

Her face softened, as if under his fists. "Oh, Mitchell. I'm sorry. I didn't knew you'd take it this hard. Why, a couple of weeks ago you told me you didn't love me anymore. I thought you didn't care." She spread her arms to him. "I guess this is what they call a reconciliation." The sleeves of the white nightgown hung, like vestments. "Come here."

For an instant, he held his ground, but then circled the bed, pulled up a chair and rested his head on her breasts, loose under the white gown. After all, he realized suddenly, he did love her.

She put her arms around him. "Mitchell, you know I wouldn't have done all these terrible, terrible things unless you seemed to be falling out of love with me. You made me so desperate."

His hand searched until it found her kneecap and began to pat it. "I know, Tam. It's all right." Far down the bed, her toes were wiggling under the blanket. Between her thighs the black needles stuck up out of the ball of pink wool.

She kissed the top of his head. "Of course, it is. Just the way it should be."

dəm

6

She kissed the top of his head again, and patted his back several times. Then Tam's mother cleared her throat. She had opened the door, and was in the room before Mitchell could sit up, take his hand away from Tam's kneecap, and smooth down his hair. He wondered if Tam had seen her enter.

"It's all right, Mitchell. We're married." Tam patted his elbow, smiled at her mother. "Hello. I didn't know you were coming up. I've been through the ordeal before."

Tam's mother stared at Mitchell, until finally he stood up and said hello, his stomach beginning to bubble.

She kissed Tam on the mouth, and sat down in Mitchell's chair. "Mitchell called me last night and he sounded so strange that I left Jake with your father and flew up. And it's a good thing I did." Her eyes were suddenly red. "Oh, my poor, poor baby. What that man must have put you through to make you do something like this!" She leaned forward, touched Tam's cheek. "I had no idea Mitchell was making you so unhappy."

"Have you seen them?" Tam knit her hands behind her head, her breasts moving upward under the white gown.

Her mother nodded. "Before I came in. And then I called your doctor to demand an explan—"

"Aren't they beautiful?"

"How can you say such a thing?" Tam's mother stood up. "And you!" She advanced on Mitchell now, her right hand raised and open. "If you had been good to her, this would never have happened."

Mitchell pulled his head into his shoulders.

"Don't hit him, Mother. It won't do him any good. He already knows what he's done."

His mother-in-law lowered her hand. "Oh, Tam, you don't know what *you've* done."

"Of course, I do, and I'm sorry. But sit down now and let's talk. You can help me decide what—"

"You mean you haven't decided yet? Why, you'll have to give it away."

Tam smiled. "Don't be silly. To whom?"

"What difference does it make?" She opened her handbag, and took out a cigaret. Mitchell, behind her chair, reached over her shoulder with a light.

Tam had been shaking her head. "I won't do it."

"Of course, you will, dear."

"I think it's a good idea, Mother. I told her . . ." He stopped when Tam's mother turned around.

"But, why not, Tam? Surely it can't mean anything to you. Especially compared to what you'll have to face."

Tam shook her head. "I've already faced it." Her fingers began to poke into the ball of wool in her lap. "Mitchell knows why all this happened. He knows that he drove me out of the house. I want to keep the baby to remind him, when we're happy again, of how unhappy we were. Now, I don't want to talk about it anymore."

Tam's mother thought for a moment, then put her hand on the bed. "You know you'll have to make at least some changes."

"Like what?" Tam was suspicious.

Her mother clicked her tongue. "Your father and I paid all that money to educate you, but sometimes I don't think you learned a thing." She shook her head. "First of all, if you're really going to keep it, you'll have to move to a larger place, perhaps a nice house out somewhere. And then you'll have to dismiss your German woman, and hire a young colored girl, an ugly dark one. Not too attractive." She turned and looked at Mitchell. "Then she can walk the babies and your new friends will assume the darker one is hers." She brightened. "It will do wonders for your reputation. Your new friends will be sure you took in this nice, ugly girl, and allowed her to keep her child with her. Now do you see what I mean? You should've at least thought of that. Sometimes I don't know what you'd do without me." She turned her cheek to Tam. "But I love you, even if sometimes you are shortsighted."

Tam kissed her, then looked at Mitchell. "Do you know any real estate men?"

"I think so." Perhaps someone at the office, who lived in the suburbs, would know something.

"You mean you don't know who you know?" Tam sucked her tongue.

"Now, Tam, don't be too hard on Mitchell." Tam's mother stood up. "He's your husband and you have to try to be nice to him. He'll do his best." She looked so deeply into his eyes that finally he had to turn away. She put her arms around him and kissed him on the side of his mouth. He could feel a hard ruby pin lodging in a space between his ribs. "He's a dear man, just like your father."

"You're embarrassing him." Tam was amused. But Mitchell was more surprised than embarrassed.

"Do I embarrass you, Mitchell?" She caught and held his eye again, hugged him tighter, swaying slightly, her knees against his shins.

"No, Mother." Strangely, the fire in his stomach was dying out.

"That's very good." She rubbed the small of his back, then released him. "Well, I just came to make sure everything was all right." She went to the bed, leaned down and kissed Tam's cheek. "Someday you'll have to tell me all about your two new babies."

Tam smiled. "I will." She thought for a moment. "How's Jake?"

"Just fine. But I'm going to keep him for three more weeks. It'll give you time to get settled, find a new girl and all. And it will certainly do him a lot of good."

"That's good. Thank you, Mother."

"It's really nothing. Besides, I want to see him grow up correctly." She kissed Tam again. "If I hurry I can get one of those shuttles back. Bye-bye." She patted Tam's arm, looked once more at Mitchell, and smiled. "Good-bye, Mitchell." He heard her hard heels in the corridor.

Her mother had left a smile on Tam's face. She looked happy, but tired. Finally, her smile sank away, water into sand, and she turned to Mitchell. "My poor dear. You must feel left out of things, like all new fathers."

He hated to acknowledge the grain of jealousy. "A little."

"Well, she's gone now. Come here to me. You're being very sweet."

As long as she recognized some of the feelings that moved inside him, everything else seemed unimportant. He sat down in the chair, and she kissed him, her lips barely parted, tight across her teeth. He found himself hoping it would not be too long before she came home.

WILLIAM MELVIN KELLEY

7

Tam's mother, her young legs crossed, sat waiting for him near the elevator on the street floor. She stood up, took his arm and led him out into the early winter wind. "This is very serious, Mitchell. I believe she really intends to keep it."

For a moment, he was too surprised to answer. His mind had seen her in a taxi heading for the airport. Now she was beside him, the top of her head at his shoulder. She was wearing a dark suit, a light green silk blouse open at her wrinkled neck. The ruby pin stood out just above where the jacket dropped straight down from the ends of her breasts. Her face was smooth and young. "Well, you certainly don't want her to keep it, do you?"

He only wanted to make up for all that he had done to her. If keeping the baby would make her happy, then she could keep it. But he wondered how to tell his mother-in-law that what she wanted would make Tam unhappy. "No, I don't. But she wants to keep it. So . . ."

She halted them in the center of the sidewalk, let go his arm. He looked at her hair, slightly gray and cut short. "Oh, Mitchell, I'm just a wretched meddling old fool." She looked up, her chin quivering. "I'm always flying up to New York to run your lives."

Halfway down the block a policeman was watching. He set his face and began toward them, swinging his brown club.

Mitchell put his arm around her shoulder. "Come on, Mother. Let's go someplace and sit down. It'll be all right." All this seemed to be bringing them closer together. His stomach rested.

She leaned against him. Though she looked very solid, Mitchell was always surprised by how soft she was. "Would you like a drink or something?" They were just passing the black window of a cocktail lounge. Before answering, she squinted through the glass at the few well-dressed couples on high stools.

"Yes, I think I'd like something." She smiled at him.

Inside, they sat in one of the booths that lined the wall. Upholstered in red leather, they were too small; no matter how he shifted he always seemed to be touching one of her knees.

A red light over her head left her face in dark red shadow. "You're being very nice to me." She shook her head. "I haven't always been very nice to you, I'm afraid."

She was telling the truth. "I don't think we've really had a chance to talk. I mean, if we had, you'd have seen how much I love Tam, how hard I try to make her happy." He looked at the red palms of his hands. "I haven't always been successful, I guess . . ."

"I know now that you want to Tam to be happy. I can see how much you're willing to endure."

He was just about to ask what she meant when the bartender came to the booth and took their order. Tam's mother wanted tea; Mitchell ordered a martini. When the bartender left, Mitchell leaned forward. "What did you mean by endure?"

She rested her hands on the small table. "Well, it's obvious that . . . the bartender wants you."

For a moment he did not understand her, then turning toward the bar, he found the bartender waving at him, small eyes in a large white face. Mitchell excused himself.

"Listen, pal, I'm not butting in." the bartender patted his shoulder. "But what kind of racket you running?"

"Racket?"

The bartender closed his eyes. "You really want the old doll to have tea? Now, I got pills and vodka's all right. No taste. But . . ." He looked at his hand, lying palm up on the bar.

Mitchell laughed quietly. "No. She's my mother-in-law."

"I know all that. But does she really get just plain tea?"

"I'm sorry. Yes, she wants tea."

The bartender shrugged, turned away. "Everybody does it different."

Mitchell returned to the booth. "He wanted to know how I wanted my martini."

She nodded. He wished he could see her face. "At any rate, Mitchell, it won't be easy. That baby will cause you a great deal of pain. You might even lose your job." Her teeth shone pink—even—slanted inward from the gum. "But there I go meddling again. You're very brave." She shifted and her knee slipped between his thighs.

WILLIAM MELVIN KELLEY

He tried to disentangle himself, but could not get far enough back into the soft, narrow seat. The bartender brought their order.

"No one at my job has to know." He was beginning to see her face now, his eyes adjusting to the light.

"But they will." She squeezed the juice of a lemon-slice into her cup. "I'm not going to say any more gloomy things. We really should celebrate. I've become a grandmother for the second and third time. You're a father for the second time." She lifted her cup. He touched it with his martini.

"It's not easy to be a mother, Mitchell." She sipped her tea, lips quivering against the heat. "First one goes through a great deal of pain to conceive, and then to give birth. Then one watches a child grow up and marry and have children of its own. And one wants to make certain the child will be happy. That doesn't seem too much to ask, does it?" She reached across the table and put her hand on top of his.

He did not want to hold her hand, but did not dare insult her by pulling away, not when they were getting along so well. "No, Mother."

"I don't think so either. Not after all the pain one can experience in a life." She returned his hand.

He wondered how much pain she had really experienced. All her life she had been at least moderately wealthy.

She must have read his face. "Pain has nothing to do with poverty. The poor, in fact, are fortunate. They have no responsibilities. If a poor woman no longer loves her husband, she simply leaves him. But the wealthy don't have that kind of freedom. At least, *we* don't."

Mitchell finished his martini, an oily drink, and beckoned to the bartender to bring another.

"*We* suffer bitterly. *We* carry the responsibility of the entire civilization." She nodded. "We are the original people. Do you understand? Without people like us, this would be a lower-class Southern European slum. There would be no civilization at all. Those people ran from civilization, from education. We didn't. The real burden of maintaining civilization falls on us, especially on our women. The men may oversee the land, but we women maintain the culture. That's what it is to be a mother, Mitchell." She patted her mouth with a napkin. "You don't really understand me, do you."

"Of course, I do, Mother." He lied.

She closed her eyes slowly, then opened them—stared at him. "Of course, you do." She leaned forward, flattening the bottoms of her breasts against the table, forcing the tops out of the neck of her blouse. "I'm hungry. Aren't you? Why don't you take me to dinner?"

8

They did not arrive home until nearly five in the morning. First, at his mother-in-law's suggestion they ate dinner at a Japanese restaurant, where girls in kimonos, soft as flowers, had prepared their food right at their table. After that Tam's mother asked him if he wanted to go dancing. "Aren't we supposed to be celebrating? Don't people dance when they celebrate?"

She did not dance well. But unlike Tam, she let him lead, standing close to him, her face serious, her eyes fixed on the knot of his tie. Mitchell even surprised himself by talking her into doing the newer dances.

At three-thirty, he realized he must be quite drunk; at the time he was sipping at his tenth martini, between puffs and bites on a dollar cigar. Tam's mother, across from him, the dance floor behind her as alive as canned worms, seemed the only peaceful person in the room. Her suit remained unwrinkled. Her green silk blouse was still fresh, though one button had come undone, and he could see the seam of what looked like a man's undershirt.

He reached out and touched her hand. "I seem drunk to you, Mother?"

"Of course not. You hold yourself very well." By mistake he blew cigar smoke into her eyes and she made a face. "But I am getting a little tired. You know, I'm not a young woman."

Through the smoke he looked at the undershirt seam, some ribbed fabric. Like Tam, her breasts were freckled. "That's not true at all."

"You're very kind, Mitchell."

They started home. In the lobby of his building, the alcohol became too heavy for Mitchell to carry alone. She supported him, his hand gripping the soft flesh under her arm. "I'm sorry, Mother. Really. I guess I had too much to drink."

"That's all right, Mitchell. You don't become a father of a Negro every day."

He gave her the key; she carried him straight to the kitchen. "I'll make you some coffee and you'll feel much better."

She sat him at the kitchen table, took off her jacket, began opening and closing cabinets, knowing where everything was kept. He would watch, then find his chin resting on the cold plastic tabletop. "I'm sloppy. I hate sloppy drunks. I'm sorry. You must think I'm a . . . a . . ."

"Now, now I don't. You're all right." She set the coffee to boil, sat across from him, staring at him. In the bright light, he could see her face much better, and the dark lines across her neck, the open green collar, the freckles. "Now you just wait here, Mitchell. I'm going to find one of Tam's nightgowns and put out your pajamas." She left the kitchen, her skirt not quite hiding the blue veins behind her knees.

The coffee began to gurgle. He watched the bubbles rising up the glass tube, spurting into the thick glass dome, turning the water brown. He wondered why until now, he and Tam's mother had not been able to get along. He had often tried to start conversations, but she had always finished them quickly. Now, perhaps their common concern for Tam had forced them to talk, to get acquainted.

"Well, how are you feeling?" The nightgown was too big for her, hanging wide at the neck, more freckles than ever, and almost to her ankles. Her feet were bare, the nails, surprisingly, painted blue. She went to the stove. "You'll have to find me a robe and some slippers later. I suppose I look indecent. But, after all, you're my son-in-law, so I suppose it doesn't matter.

Mitchell clamped his knees together, ashamed. "Of course not."

"I'll have your coffee in a moment." She had to stand on the tips of her blue toes to reach the cups. Finally she brought the steaming coffee and sat across from him.

"Thank you, Mother." It had been years since Tam had cooked anything for him. He mentioned it.

"That's because you're too kind. You don't ask her to do it, do you?"

He shook his head. "She always refused, so finally I stopped asking." The coffee was warming his stomach, but the steam rising into his nostrils, clouded his mind. Then he heard himself say: "All this isn't my fault just alone. A lot of it is. I know that. I really do. But I tried my best. I'll never be a millionaire, but I tried to be good to her." He wiped his nose with his palm. "But I guess it wasn't good enough."

"Now, don't, Mitchell." She stretched out her hand to him.

He looked at it and continued: "Sometimes I just want to go back into the Service, and fight in one of the wars. Then I'd know I was being useful. I wasn't a great soldier, but I tried to do my best." He shook his head. "And now she runs out and sleeps with a nigger. A nigger! Not even a white man. If it had been a white man, I might never have known." He shut his eyes, trying to keep the water inside.

He felt her hands on his shoulder. Opening his eyes, he saw nothing but the soft gauze of the nightgown. "Now, now, Mitchell. Let Mother tell you what to do." The squares of gauze grew bigger, covering his face. He put his arms around her, pulled her to him as he used to do when his own mother came to rescue him from the little men who pecked at his eyes with ice picks. He rested his forehead in the triangle just below, between her breasts. "Now, now."

She lowered herself slowly onto his lap, and kissed his mouth gently. "Let Mother tell you what you must do if you want Tam to love you."

He looked at her face now; it was kind and smiling, a mother's face. She patted his cheek.

"She's my daughter, Mitchell, and I know her. Sometimes, for her own good, I've had to force her to do things. I couldn't just let her have her own way all the time. Now, she wants to keep that child. And you're ready to let her, aren't you, because you think it will make her happy. But you know that it won't make her happy, don't you."

He nodded. "But what—"

She stopped him with another kiss. "Dear, Mitchell, let me tell you what. You must find out who the father is. Then—"

"She already told me. I know who he is."

"Good." She shifted on his lap, soft, and not at all heavy. "Now you must go to him. And you must convince him to take the child. It won't be difficult. He probably loves Tam and wants her to be happy." She put cold fingers to his mouth. "I know it's hard to accept that another man loves your wife. But it's not any more difficult than accepting that she's had his child. But what does it matter really? She couldn't have any feeling for him. She doesn't have any feeling for the child. She just feels that since she went through all that pain, she must have something to show for it. You thank God that you'll never have to bring a child into the world." She smiled. "Now does that make sense to you? Of course it does. You see, Mitchell, something like this could completely ruin your life. You don't know that because in New York it doesn't happen very often. But in Washington, we've had more experience and know what to do. All this must seem difficult, I know, especially doing something Tam doesn't want done. But you must be man enough to do it. You must make up your own mind and act on your decision. Now, isn't Mother right?"

He had to admit that she was, and told her so.

"That's a good boy." She put her arm around his neck, hugged him, kissed his cheek. "Now, you go get ready for bed and I'll come and say good night." She climbed off his lap.

She had turned down the spread, put clean pajamas on the pillow. He undressed and got into bed. He missed Tam's weight on the other side. In a while, Tam's mother knocked and came in. She leaned over and kissed him. His eyes closed on a milky way of freckles.

He slept until four the next afternoon. Wetting his numbed tongue, he read the note she had left on the bed table:

Dear Mitchell:

Filled with respect for my son-in-law, I'm taking an early plane back to Washington. I have always known you were a good man. Now I realize that you are also a strong man. You have decided to do the right thing. I'm very proud of you.

Love, Mother

9

To find this Cooley, the Black baby's father, he knew he would have to contact Opal Simmons. After dressing, he began to search for her address and number. Tam, very organized for a woman, saved everything. Among the envelopes containing the sports-clothes receipts, a letter from her dressmaker asking for payment, old airline tickets, the nursery school bill, the canceled checks, and deposit slips, he finally found Opal's address.

He went to the phone and dialed her number, knowing that this conversation would not be pleasant, for either of them. He could only remind Opal that Tam had taken from her a man she may have loved. And then there was the whole business of her stealing. Though he had never asked her, she must have had good reason to risk job and reputation. And she must have sold everything quickly, for cash; he had never found any of it in her possession, had never even been certain what she had taken. But for good reason or no, he knew she would not enjoy speaking again to the person who had exposed her.

Opal picked up her phone after the third ring. "Hello?"

He did not know where to begin. He tried to announce himself, but could not. Before he realized it, he had quietly slipped the receiver back into its cradle. "Hell—"

He sat at the phone table wondering why he had been unable to give even his name. After all, he and Opal were not strangers; she had worked for them eighteen months. Suddenly—her name and number in front of him—he remembered that once he had driven her home, to a project in the north Bronx, countless tall red buildings, surrounded by patches of yellow grass. He had been unable to speak on that drive, though, hating silence, he always tried to fill it. In his apartment, they had talked about hundreds of things, what Jake had done during the day, or how well she cooked, or whether one of his suits had been returned from the cleaners. But that night in the car, just as a few minutes before on the phone, he could not speak.

He stood up, finally convincing himself that it did not really matter. It was probably better not to have spoken to her. She might have refused to see him. Now he knew she was at home. He would drive to the Bronx and speak to her in person.

It was nearly six when he reached the highway; there were few cars. Even so, after a moment or two, he found himself being pursued through the November dusk by two white headlights, could feel their heat on his neck. He tried to look for a face, a cloth hat with a wire frame, but the car was almost invisible above the lights. He sped up, but the lights stayed with him, exploding in his mirror.

Then the road ahead was filled with small red lights, which spread across his windshield. The cars, bunched now, began to move to the right. He passed a splintered wooden pole, then the aluminum lamp shades, mashed and wrinkled like foil. He had to swerve to avoid an arm, and the steering wheel its hand still clutched. The first car rested partly on the grass divide, a wheel quiet beside it. The second car was on its back. A Black man sat in the driver's seat of the third car.

A Black woman sat beside it, on the grass, her feet in the highway. She must have weighed two hundred pounds, one huge breast in a white bra hanging through a rip in her flowered dress. She had not tried to cover it; her hands lay palms up on her thighs. She wore only one shoe; a large yellow hat, crushed now, the cloth flowers torn, rested in the grass next to her. She was shaking her head.

Once he had passed it all, the road again open before him, Mitchell too shook his head. Some people, he thought, ought not to be allowed to get licenses. It was too easy for the reckless to get them. It was that way with many things. Some people worked very hard, earning their way; others hitched rides—holding up those who had been nice enough to pick them up. As he turned off the highway, and passed a large cemetery, he thought he was beginning to understand what Tam's mother had been trying to tell him.

WILLIAM MELVIN KELLEY

10

In twenty more minutes, he parked his car. On the sidewalk, three young Black men stopped talking as he climbed out. They watched him roll up his windows, lock and check his doors, securing his car against theft. He made a wide circle around them, started up a walk leading to four buildings. He stayed to the side of the walk, his knee grazing the chain which protected the dead yellow grass from children.

In front of the first building, a group of small Black girls were arguing in high little voices. One had a long rope. "It's your turn to hold, Gail."

"No, it ain't. It's Wanda's turn."

"See that? See that? I ain't your friend if you don't hold."

Gail, head divided into neat squares of hair, took the rope. Another girl held the other end. Just before Mitchell reached them, the girls began to jump, over two strands, each looping in opposite directions. He could not get by them, and had to wait.

Sitting in a teepee, smoking a pipe.
Polar bear come with a great big knife.
Polar bear take and put us in a boat.
So many children, thing couldn't float.
Sitting in a boat, with a necklace of iron.
Bear come down and say, "You're mine."
Children started crying, raise up a noise.
Everybody's crying, even the boys.

The jumping girl sang the loudest, her skirt billowing around thin black legs, the ribbons in her hair following her up and down. All the girls looked cold, their dark skin filmed with ashes.

Sitting in a cabin, smoking a pipe.
The polar bear say I his wife.
Take me by the hand and lead me out.
Bear in the grass with a big cold snout.

Sitting in a cabin, apron up high.
So homesick I wish I could die....

The jumping girl tripped on the ropes, and the other girls began to laugh. Then they were all staring at Mitchell, mouths poked out.

"You a child molasses?" the girl called Gail asked.

He took a step backward and asked for Opal's building.

They held a short conference, then pointed toward the last building in the row, and permitted him to pass. His neck muscles did not relax until the ropes began again to slap the pavement and he heard them chanting.

By then he had reached the lobby, was wading through the contents of a broken bag of garbage, avoiding a gravy-filled grapefruit shell, fat oozing from a green soda bottle. He pressed the elevator button.

"Sure you got the right place?" A brown man in a blue imitation policeman's uniform tapped him on the shoulder with his club. He was shorter than Mitchell, graying around the ears, with a neat little mustache.

Mitchell nodded, his back against the elevator door.

"For your own protection, you know. Better make sure you mean to be here." He struck his palm lightly.

"I'm visiting Miss Opal Simmons."

The imitation policeman smiled. "I ain't going to ask what for. You got business here, all right. I'm just thinking about people come around making trouble." He paused. "The people I work for pays me to keep things calm, nice and calm."

"I'm calm. Really."

"Sure." He nodded. "I can see that. It's for your own protection. When you go back put in a good word for me. Tell them I'm keeping things calm." Mitchell started to ask where the imitation policeman thought he was returning to, but was cut off: "Your elevator's here." And bowing slightly, the imitation policeman opened the door for him.

WILLIAM MELVIN KELLEY

11

The elevator banged up the shaft, and Mitchell stepped out into a long gray hall, lit by one bulb in a broken glass globe. He found Opal's apartment, rang the bell, and, after a moment, a small barred hole opened in the door. "Yes?"

He put his mouth close to the bars. "Opal, it's Mr. Pierce."

The little round hole closed, locks clicked, the big door opened. Opal's eyes seemed as large as the door-hole. "Mr. Pierce?"

"Hello, Opal. How are you?"

"Fine, Mr. Pierce." She pulled the door wider, asked him to come in, please, as if once again she were answering his door. He crossed the doorsill, wondering why she was being so nice.

The living room was small, strangely familiar. The sofa was green, plastic-covered. A light brown coffee table squatted in front of it. On the wall was one picture, a reproduction of a painting by a famous modern Spanish artist. Opal asked him to sit down. He did, under the reproduction; she sat across from him, in a red chair, also plastic-covered, also familiar.

He cleared his throat. "How've you been, Opal?"

"Fine. And you, Mr. Pierce?" She had gained a great deal of weight. Her legs, pressed tightly together at the knee, were still shapely. But her shoulders had taken on a thick padding of fat, which spilled down her arms as far as her elbows. He remembered he had always worried about her eating too much rice.

"Fine." He tried to think of something more to say, but could not. It did not matter. She seemed so nervous it put him at ease. "Listen, Opal, I want you to do me a favor."

She leaned forward, a smile pulling at her lips. "Sure, Mr. Pierce."

He took a deep breath. "I'd like to find your friend Cooley." He watched closely for her reaction, saw a tear pop into her eye. "Opal?"

"He cause you more trouble, Mr. Pierce? I'm sorry I ever brought him to your house. Of all the men I ever met, he was the most trouble-causing . . ." She shook her head.

"Wait a minute, Opal."

"That man was a jinx." She looked at him, a tear stalled on her cheek, like brown wax. "Why'd you fire me, Mr. Pierce? It was for going around with men like Cooley, wasn't it."

"Now, Opal . . ."

"The best job I ever had and I lost it because of a common, ordinary nigger. Excuse me, Mr. Pierce, but we both know what he was." She wiped her tears with a chubby hand. "A nigger."

"No, Opal." Mitchell shook his head. "We fired you because you were stealing. That's why I went through your purse. Don't you remember?"

"Me?" She sat up, snorted. "I never stole from you, Mr. Pierce. Not even leftover food. My pay check was always enough."

Mitchell suddenly realized that at very least she believed what she was telling. Either she had forgotten or had gone insane. He was certain he would know if she was lying. "No, Opal, you were stealing from us."

"What kind of person would I be to steal from you, as good as you was to me?"

He had often wondered that himself. "But, Opal . . ." He stopped because he knew now why the living room seemed so familiar; it was a poor copy of his own—designed by Tam—even to the reproduction.

"What did I steal, Mr. Pierce?"

He hesitated. "Well, Opal, I don't really know." That too seemed strange; they had never really missed anything. He tried to remember why he had even believed Opal to be a thief.

"You see?" She was triumphant, but not angry. "It was because of that Cooley. You were right to fire me, Mr. Pierce. I never should've had that nigger come to your house. I didn't even like him. I only went out with him three times." She stopped. "What you want him for, Mr. Pierce?"

The idea that Opal had not stolen from them had, for the moment, pushed Cooley from his head. "I want him to do a favor for me."

"He won't do nothing for you, Mr. Pierce. He's too evil. You stay away from him."

"No. I have to see him." He looked at her, saw her old thin face encased in fat, like one balloon inside another. "Listen, Opal, I guess I made a mistake about firing you." He nodded. "How would you like to come work for us again?"

WILLIAM MELVIN KELLEY

Her mouth became the top of a brown jar. "Me? Work for you again? Even after what I done?"

"We'll forget that." He smiled. "We want you to work for us. I can give you, oh say, twenty dollars more a month than you were making before. You see, Mrs. Pierce just had a baby, and she'll need help."

"A new baby? And how's my old baby, Jakie? I'd love to work for you. And I promise never to go out with any nigger like Cooley again."

"Good." He paused. "Now, where can I find him? By the way, Opal, what's his last name?"

"God, Mr. Pierce, I don't know. He never told me. I ain't even seen him in a year and a half. Like I tell you, I didn't go out with him but three times. But I met him by my nephew. His name's Carlyle . . . Bedlow. He may know where Cooley's at." She got up, and, bending over a small desk, huge buttocks filling the room, wrote down her nephew's address. "He only lives a few blocks from here."

He told her to come to work in two days—enough time for him to dismiss the German woman, whom he had never liked. If Tam did not approve, he could say he was following her mother's advice. Besides, Opal was no longer attractive.

Downstairs, walking to his car, he felt so good that he was not even nervous when he passed the jumping, chanting Black girls.

12

It was full dark now. Steering his car around great holes in the tattered streets, it was hard for Mitchell to believe he was still in New York City. He passed shadowed swamplike lots, glimpsed a goat in his headlights. In places, there were no sidewalks.

Opal's nephew lived in one of a row of attached, three-story brick houses. Each owner had tried to make his house distinctive. One had a white picket fence and green awnings, another an iron fence and red awnings. But still, it remained one long building, with four or five entrances.

Mitchell pressed the button under the name—BEdLow. The buzzer rang; he pushed open the door, stepped into a dark, cold hallway, and crept forward until he came to a stairway—then light.

"How do you go, Brother?" A young man's voice.

"Hello?" Mitchell shouted. "What did you say?" He started climbing clean rubber-covered stairs, heard footsteps coming to meet him. He had almost gained a small landing, when the young man appeared around a corner.

"A devil?" The young man, in his late teens, was short, heavy eyebrows over brown eyes, embedded in an otherwise hairless dark-brown head. "What you want, devil?"

Mitchell stopped. "Are you Carlyle Bedlow?"

The young man did not answer, turned, and started back up the stairs. "A devil for you, Carlyle!"

Mitchell followed timidly, turned the corner, found another young man standing in a doorway, staring down at him. He was older than the first, his skin as dark, a mustache hiding his upper lip, his hair long—and straight? "What you want?"

Clearing his throat, Mitchell gave his name. "Your aunt, Opal Simmons, sent me over."

The young man nodded. "Yeah?"

"I'm trying to find a friend of hers, and yours? named Cooley." Looking up was making his neck ache.

"Cooley? Cooley what? Sorry, Mr. Pierce. I don't think I know no

Cooley." The young man was wearing a knit sport shirt, tight pants. "What're you to my A'nt Opal?"

Mitchell explained that some two years before Opal had worked for him, and, beginning Monday, would work for him again.

While he talked, the young man lit a cigaret. "Yeah, I remember being told about you. You fired her for stealing, right? Yeah. A'nt Opal stealing, that's funny as all shit."

Mitchell nodded. "It was a misunderstanding. That's why I rehired her."

"Oh, I see it now. That's real nice. Cooley. I think I know him after all. So you want to find Cooley, huh?" He stepped back into the apartment. "Come on up. I ain't seen him in a while, but . . ."

Mitchell reached the top step, climbed into the apartment. The young man reached out his hand. "Carlyle Bedlow, Junior. Carlyle."

"Nice to know you." Mitchell took his hand.

"Come on in my room." Carlyle closed the door and started toward the front of the apartment. Mitchell followed, looking over his shoulder, where a lighted doorway had attracted his attention. The first young man was sitting at a desk in a little room, reading. On the floor were piles of books and magazines, on the wall, a portrait, in color, of a black, fat-faced man with long kinky hair, his eyes hidden by blue, gold-rimmed sunglasses.

"That's Mance, my brother." Carlyle had not turned his head. "He trying to find a way to kill you." They entered a room, lit only by an orange bulb.

Mitchell felt a pain in his chest. "Me?"

"White people, man. He's a Jesuit. You know, a Black Jesuit?" He sat down, sighing, in the room's only chair. "Reads all the time. Looking for a way." He laughed, a snort. "May find it too. Close the door." Mitchell did—after one more look at Mance, bent over his studies.

Mitchell came from the door; the room was too small. "But why does he want to kill all white people?"

Carlyle watched him a moment, then motioned for him to sit on the bed. "I guess because you need it; he's an idealist. You want some Smoke?"

"No, thanks. I have some cigarets."

"Yeah, okay." He blinked, rubbed his eyes. "So, why you want to find Cooley, Mr. Pierce?"

"Well, if you don't mind I'd rather not say." Then to put Carlyle at ease. "But it's not anything illegal, if you're worried about that."

Carlyle sat up straighter. "I'm glad you said that, Mr. Pierce. I sure don't like to get involved in nothing E-legal."

Mitchell, still wearing his overcoat, was beginning to sweat. "Can you help me?"

"That's hard to say, Mr. Pierce. Like I say, I ain't seen Cooley for a while and he moves around a lot." He opened a drawer in a little table beside his chair, took out a package of cigaret paper and a bottle filled with greenish tobacco. "It's imported, man. Very strong, smells like hell. How soon you want to find him?"

"As soon as I can."

Carlyle poured some of the green tobacco into the paper, rolled a thin cigaret, and lit it. It did smell bad. "You see, that's the thing. Could cost some money."

Mitchell was becoming suspicious. He had read about white men swindled by Black. He would be cautious, careful. "How do you mean?"

"You got a car?" Mitchell nodded. "Well, we could get in your car, drive to Harlem, and go some places he might be. But we might have to pay admission and like that. And . . . I think I should warn you, man, Cooley's kind of an underworld figure. A lot of people'd look at you and think you was a cop, and we'd have to give them some money to get them to talk. You understand?"

"I see." This seemed reasonable enough. "I think I have money for that."

Carlyle shrugged. "I want to be honest with you." He patted his chest. "I mean, there a lot of bad feelings between the races. Like with my brother. But me? I don't go for it. A man is a man, and I don't kid no man. So I got to warn you: we might spend some money and never find him or anything about him."

Mitchell was moved by Carlyle's honesty. "Well, I hope we do find him, but if we don't, I'll know you tried to help me."

Carlyle stood up. "You a good man, Mr. Pierce. I guess I should've known that by the way you took A'nt Opal back after that misunderstanding." He went to his closet and put on a wine-colored sport coat. "So, I guess we better start."

"Good."

They left the room; Carlyle stopped at the front door. "Say, Mance, I'm cutting. I'll catch you later."

Mance looked up from his book, nodded.

Mitchell smiled. "Good-bye, now."

"Devil."

13

Outside, under a streetlamp, Carlyle suggested it might be easier if he drove; he would not have to direct Mitchell through the Harlem streets. "Besides, man, there's this race business." He winked. "They won't wreck your car if they see me get from behind the wheel." Mitchell asked to see his license, and, satisfied they would not be breaking the law, surrendered the keys.

Because Carlyle knew the Bronx streets, they were soon on the highway. They passed the place where, not three hours before, Mitchell had seen the accident. The cars and people were gone; only the splintered pole marked the spot. They climbed a short hill and in front of him, Mitchell saw the tall, light-barnacled shadows of the city.

He was beginning to relax now, growing accustomed to the way Carlyle drove his car. He felt certain he would find Cooley and be rid of the baby before the evening was over. He slid down, his head on the seat, and tried to remember how Cooley had looked that night eighteen months before, the only time Mitchell had ever seen him.

He had been sitting at the kitchen table, enjoying the smell of the apple pie Opal had baked for him. She had just left the room, Jake in her arms, his hand inside the neck of her dress, his fingers tugging on the strap of her bra. Then the buzzer, and he had opened the door.

First, Mitchell had noticed Cooley's nose, as if the heel of a hand had jammed the end of it back and up toward his small, red eyes, and held it there, stretching the nostrils to the size of black quarters. The upper lip had been three fingers wide, the lower lip drooping, pink—all this packed onto a head no larger, it almost seemed, than a softball, and that sitting, neckless, on shoulders the width of the door. The shoulders and chest had been covered by a chartreuse jacket, with the name— Cooley—in gold thread over the heart. He had looked down at Mitchell almost from the top of the doorway. "Who are you?"

He had not allowed Cooley to intimidate him. "Mitchell Pierce," he had answered deliberately. "And just who are you?"

"Cooley." Challenged, he seemed to shrink a bit. "I come for Opal."

Already, Mitchell had begun to get angry, but before he could

WILLIAM MELVIN KELLEY

answer, Opal had entered the kitchen. And then the rest of it. He had demanded that Cooley wait outside, had begun to reprimand her, had called her a thief, had dismissed her. It was clear now what had happened; anger had confused him. He had attacked Opal because of Cooley's rudeness . . .

They crossed a bridge, the tires howling on hivelike steel, and stopped next to a big, new car carrying a Black man and two brown girls, one of them under blond, almost white hair. Carlyle elbowed him. "Roll down the window."

Mitchell did, and Carlyle lay across his lap, that straight, oily hair, sweet-smelling just under his nose. The roots were not at all straight. "Hey, baby, where you going?"

The blond turned toward him, scowled. The man smiled. "Sorry, bubba, all for me."

"Go on, man, she don't need no translator."

The blond smiled, but turned away.

"Listen, I'll tell you what—you meet me at the Apple-O at midnight, I'll take you to the show. You can get rid of them people."

The blond was still smiling. "I seen it already, baby. Besides, I meet you and my man'll beat hell out of me. Won't you, honey?" She leaned over and kissed the man. Behind them, horns started, and the car disappeared up a ramp, its back red with lights.

"Okay, Mr. Pierce, roll up." Carlyle stepped on the gas, and they started down Seventh Avenue.

"Isn't it dangerous to talk like that to another man's wife?"

"Ain't no other man; that's my Brother."

Mitchell did not understand, but did not dwell on it. Cooley still loomed in his mind. He wondered now, as the dead trees on the narrow center strip whipped by, how Tam had ever met him. Someday, but not soon, he would ask her. Opal had said she had gone out with him only three times. Probably the night of the misunderstanding had been the last time.

Cooley had probably come to the house before that, seen Tam, and had decided he loved her.

Perhaps he had come late one morning, after the German woman had taken Jake to the park. Tam would have been in bed, napping, reading, watching television, when the doorbell rang:

The German woman, Tam thinks, has forgotten her key. She gets up and goes to the door, not bothering to cover her pink, freckled shoulders, the white lace. She opens the door.

Cooley stands in the hall, his large black hands buried in dark pockets. "I like to see Opal for a minute. I'm Cooley."

At first Tam is frightened, but if Cooley knows Opal, it is probably safe. "Opal doesn't work here anymore."

His eyes blink. "Oh . . ."

Now Tam realizes he is looking through the lace, but he does not leer; there is an innocence about him. He has been expecting to see Opal. Now he is a disappointed child. She asks him in, runs to get a robe.

When she returns to the living room, he is on the edge of the small antique chair, afraid to put his full weight on the twisted legs, awed by the tranquillity of the room she has designed.

She sits across from him on the sofa. "Do you know Opal well?"

"No, ma'am, I only been out with her three times." He finds it hard to look at her.

"So she didn't tell you she's not working here anymore?"

He shakes his tiny black head. He cannot sustain it, cannot lie to her; he must look at her, confess. "I seen you before, Mrs. Pierce, one time when I come for Opal. I ain't been able to think of nothing else. I can't work; I can't sleep. And now today I come down here and asks for Opal. I know Opal don't work here no more." He drops from the chair to his knees. "But I figured I'd come to the door and ask for her, just on the chance of seeing you." The knuckles of his black hands sink into the rug; he begins to crawl toward her, the chartreuse satin, like skin across his shoulders. "Just to see you. But then you was kind enough to ask me into your house. I ain't never seen a house this nice."

Tam slides back onto the sofa. "Please, Cooley."

"I ain't going to hurt you, Mrs. Pierce. I wouldn't do that." Over her knees, she can see only his small red eyes. His hands grip her ankles. "I loves you, Mrs. Pierce." Her feet are growing numb, cold, even so, she can feel his lips just behind her toes.

She should jump up, scream, but does not. She thinks of Mitchell, who no longer loves her, who does not appreciate her. They are arguing.

WILLIAM MELVIN KELLEY

And now Opal's Cooley has come to her, and, demanding nothing, has confessed honest, childlike love for her. She begins to unbutton her robe.

But she never finishes. By her ankles, he pulls her off the sofa, bouncing her soft buttocks to the rug. He tears at the robe. Pink, cloth-covered buttons pop and fly. And now the freckles under white lace seem to madden him. He pulls at the lace, destroys the knitted cobwebs.

She lies still, beginning to cry, thinking, Mitchell, Mitchell, see what you've driven me to do . . .

"First stop, Mr. Pierce." Carlyle had parked in a dark, litter-strewn street. Down at the corner were the lights of an avenue, a bar window turning the gray pavement yellow. The houses were old, Victorian, their entrances guarded by stone dragons, angels with chipped noses. "There's a party here he might be at."

Mitchell continued to see Tam, as still as rags, spread under Cooley's shadow. He tried to shake them out of his head.

"You still want to find him?" The streetlamp caught the hard wave in Carlyle's hair.

Mitchell sat up, reached for the door handle. "Of course I do. More than ever."

14

They descended steps to a cellar doorway, passed rows of steel garbage cans. Already Mitchell could hear music. Carlyle pushed open a door into a stone hallway. "Listen, Mr. Pierce, don't say nothing. You let me talk." He winked. "This race business." They stopped and Carlyle rang the bell. "And if you don't mind, I'd better call you Mitchell."

The door opened a crack, then all the way. "Hiya, Carlyle!" Mitchell could not see her face, only tight pink slacks, a yellow turtleneck sweater, red hair, and plump arms, each with a charm bracelet, rushing to embrace Carlyle. "How you doing?"

"All right." His hand stroked the pink slacks. "You miss me?"

"Sure did." She pulled back from him, gold teeth smiling in a copper face. "And just where you been?"

"Around." Carlyle's forehead was greasy.

The gold disappeared behind lavender lips, her face serious now. "You ain't been up state, has you?"

"Nothing like that, Glora." He smiled. "Just hustling."

"Well, come in and party." From behind a hard face, she looked at Mitchell. "What's this?" scolding Carlyle with her eyes.

"You see that, Mitchell?" Carlyle shook his head. "White skin and she act like a red skin." He sucked his tongue. "This my cousin, Mitchell, from Canada. From a small, snowy-ass town where the underground railway left his granddaddy's butt. Had to integrate to keep the blood moving."

She smiled at Mitchell now, gold teeth in the dim light. "Cousin!" He felt her arms around him, red hair in his face, high breasts just above his stomach. "Welcome home. I'm sorry I took you for Sir Charles, the White Knight."

"That's all right." Mitchell did not know if he liked being . . . colored.

"What we standing out here for when they partying inside?" She hugged Mitchell's arm, pulled him over the marble doorsill, and took his coat.

"You got a cover, man," Carlyle whispered. "Just don't dance.

They know you a phoney for sure if you get on that floor."

Mitchell nodded, slightly offended. He had always considered himself a good dancer, especially when he was drunk.

Carlyle was still at his ear. "Listen, they trying to pay the Jew, so lay something on them."

"What?" The hallway was dark, a door at the end, lit red. The music came from the doorway, and inside the room, Mitchell could see shadows weaving.

"It's a rent party, so drop two dollars in the basket. A dollar a drink, and if you hungry, she got her mama making chicken and potato salad, a dollar a plate."

Glora was back, hugging his arm again. "I'm taking over your cousin, Carlyle." As if to consolidate her claim, she put her hand on Carlyle's stomach, and pushed him away.

"I'll see you later, man." Before Mitchell could protest, Carlyle winked and left them.

Glora pulled him into the room where Black people danced, nodding heads, jerking hips, feet scraping on the wooden floor. Some of the men were sweating under the red light, patting their faces with neatly folded handkerchiefs. The women's faces were stern above their dancing bodies. Mitchell had never seen a group of Black people dance before, and was surprised to find no one writhing on the floor, none of the women with skirts hitched to their waist. Everyone did the same step, moved the same way in time to the music. Even so, they seemed to be having a good time.

Around the dancers, at the edges of the room, others stood talking. In the closest group to him, a half-dozen men, and a few women stood listening, their eyes downcast, but no one seemed to be talking. Glora led him toward them.

"Well look what the cat drug in," one of the women said. "What's that, Glora?"

"This is Carlyle Bedlow's cousin from Canada. Mitchell. Don't he look white though?" She introduced him around, ". . . and down there is Shorty."

Out of the shadows in the center of their small circle reached a yellow hand. Mitchell looked down at a pinched face under a pile of straight yellow hair. The midget wore a tuxedo, a lace-front shirt. "Glad to meet you." He mashed Mitchell's knuckles. "Where from in Canada?" His voice was high, forced through tiny nostrils.

Mitchell answered that he was from a small town near Ottawa.

"That's a long way from home. I ain't never worked there." He stared at Mitchell a moment longer, almost suspiciously, then turned to the others. "Anyway, like I say, I didn't really want to join, but I like testing them. So I look up the name in the phone book: The Little Folks Club, downtown, and walks in there one day, with my Great Dane and my two-foot cane. They had like kindergarten furniture, everything low down on the floor. There's this blond at the reception desk, maybe two-six, nice body on her. I asks if I could join up. She look at me like she ain't never seen a midget before, then at my dog, and runs on into the inner sanctum and in a minute she comes out with this official-looking cat. He wearing a little Ivy League suit with a vest and these big glasses. He tried all kinds of ways to tell me they didn't allow no niggers to join, and I play it dumb, asking questions, twisting his mind around, letting my dog lick his face. Finally I asks him how short you got to be to join. He say they didn't let no one in who taller than three feet. I look him in the eye, calm and quiet as you please, then shouts, 'Three feet? Why, man, that's discrimination! I'm afraid I couldn't join no club with such an unfair policy. Some of the best midgets I know is three-foot-one!' And I jumps up on my dog's back and rides out of there. That's Charles for you!"

Only Mitchell did not laugh. Bigotry was not to him a laughing matter. The rest spun with laughter, hiding their faces on each other's shoulders.

"Say, you is out of it," Glora whispered, then kissed his ear. "Come on, I'll teach you the New York way." She embraced him.

The music had turned slow—a high tenor over a rumble. Couples stood still on the floor, their arms around each other. Mitchell wanted to pull away, but knew he had to pretend; anything to find Cooley.

"Tell me about Canada." He could just hear her above the music. Her breasts were not at all hard. He began to sweat.

"It's cold and there's a lot of snow."

"Ooooh." She squeezed him tighter. There was perfume in her hair. Suddenly, he wanted to bury his face in it, kiss her scalp, but was afraid.

WILLIAM MELVIN KELLEY

And now he could feel himself getting excited, was afraid of that too.

"Listen, before I forget, I want to pay." He pushed her away.

She shook her head. "Mitchell, you been with white people too damn long. You don't even know how to relax—all tied up in knots, thinking about money. This the weekend, man."

She took his hand and led him to the door, pointed: "My mama's in the kitchen. Pay her." She was angry. "And while you're there, get a couple drinks in you. That's the way white folks do, ain't it? Can't have a good time until they get drunk and start breaking things." She shook her head again. "Sometimes I think the Jesuits is right. I seen more good niggers ruined by integration!"

15

It was only a few steps to the kitchen. Just inside the door, a table blocked the way, a money-filled saucepan in the center. Behind the table, the kitchen was a high-ceilinged room. At one time it had been some bright color. Now it was impossible to tell what color; no one would have chosen the gray which covered the walls.

At the far end was a spattered white stove, crouching hidden behind a Black woman at least as tall and twice as wide as Mitchell. She wore a black dress decorated with large yellow sunflowers, one of which stretched across her broad back, like the picture on a team jacket.

"Is this where I pay?"

"No place else, baby." She turned now, smoke rising from an iron kettle behind her. She was the woman he had seen sitting beside the highway.

"Well?" She moved toward the table. "Ain't you got change?" She stood behind the table, large hands hanging at her sides. "It's in the pan there. Go on, I trust you."

"Didn't I see you a few hours ago on the highway?"

She wrinkled her tiny nose. "Highway?"

Perhaps he was mistaken. But . . . "You look very familiar to me."

"I ain't never been to Canada."

Mitchell was confused, decided to let the matter drop. "Is this where I pay?"

"That's what I said. Don't you light-skinned niggers never listen to anybody but white folks?"

"Why, yes." He took a five-dollar bill from his wallet. "And could I have three drinks. Do you have bourbon?"

"Course I do." She bent into a cabinet, brought out the bottle. "Three?" She squinted at him.

Perhaps three drinks were too many. "Yes." He wanted them all himself; they might relax him. "One's a double."

She poured the drinks, using a jigger glass with a thick bottom. "What's wrong now?"

"Not a thing."

"What's wrong with you, boy? You a *retard*?" She did not wait for his answer, but returned to the stove, picked up a two-pronged fork, began to spear each piece of chicken, bringing it close to her face for inspection.

He choked down a large swallow. "It's just that I think I've seen you before."

Her back to him: "I probably look like your mama."

Mitchell smiled, almost laughed. His mother, dead now eight years, had been small and dry. "No, that's not it." He took another swallow. The alcohol could not possibly be in his arteries yet, but knowing it was on its way made him feel better. "But—"

"I get one of you at every party Glora gives." She spun around. "You light-skinned, educated boys! Young Black girls scare you, so you come out and talk to mammy."

Mitchell tried not to laugh. "Really, that's not—"

"Well, mammy's a girl too and she ain't got time for scared boys." She smiled suddenly. "Unless you want to come on in the kitchen with me." She shook her head. "No, you don't want that. Go on away from here. Mammy ain't got no time no more for scared boys. Mammy wants men!"

Mitchell finished the double bourbon. "I'm not afraid."

"Then why you hanging around the kitchen?" She advanced on him, pointing the prongs of her fork at his eyes. "Go on now."

He backed away, into the darkness of the hall, and wandered, paper cup in hand, toward the dancing room. Glora was on the floor, moving inside her pink slacks. He stared at her, growing more confident all the time, certain that even across the room she would be able to feel what he was thinking about her. But she did not turn from her partner.

He stepped onto the floor, to cut in, but at that moment, saw Carlyle in a far corner talking to another man, their foreheads nearly touching. He came up behind them. "Hi, Carlyle."

"We was just talking about you." He put his arm around the other man's shoulder. "Here's a man who knows where you can find Cooley. Ain't that right, Calvin."

Calvin nodded. He was Mitchell's height and very dark, with pouches under his eyes, a thin mustache below his sharp nose. His hair was short, neatly parted. He was wearing a dark suit and white shirt. He too looked familiar, but Mitchell had to admit now that he did not know enough Black people to be able to tell them apart. He had always considered this a cliché, but realized now that it was at least partly true.

Carlyle told him that Calvin's last name was Johnson. Mitchell shook his hand, rough and cracked, but with a weak grip. "So what's happening?"

"Happening? Oh, nothing. You know Cooley?"

Calvin nodded. "I ain't seen him in about a week, but I'm pretty sure I know where he is. Carlyle says you ain't telling why you want to see him."

Mitchell realized now that, given Black people's fear and suspicion, his not telling his reasons could make it difficult to find Cooley. "You see, it's kind of private. I . . ."

"Ain't planning to kill him, are you?"

"Me?" Calvin was not joking. "No. I just want to talk to him."

"You understand my position, don't you? I wouldn't want to set up a friend of mine for a killing."

This talk of murder made Mitchell uneasy. "Sure, I know that."

"Good." He turned to Carlyle, smiled, then his tired eyes were on Mitchell again. "But I hope you won't be offended if I don't trust you for a while. I seen squarer-looking killers than you. So we'll just hang out and if you seem like you telling the truth, then maybe I'll take you to see Cooley. That sound all right to you?"

"Sure, but I really don't want to hurt him." He did not like the pleading in his voice, tried to harden it. "There may be some money in it for him."

"Okay. But if the deal's a good one, it'll keep, now won't it."

"I guess so." Mitchell was beginning to wonder whether it might be better just to forget about finding Cooley. He could force Tam to give the baby to an adoption agency. Her mother would help him. He did not at all like the people he was meeting.

Calvin smiled at him. "I know you want to find him. And I'll help you. But Cooley and me is close, and got to stick together. The business we in, can't take no chances."

Mitchell nodded.

"Carlyle tells me you like Glora a little bit." He leaned closer. "What say you take Glora; Carlyle and me'll get us some ladies, and we can go over to a place I know of and drink up some liquor and . . . see what happens. It got lots of guest rooms."

Mitchell was about to refuse, but Calvin turned him around so that he could see Glora's pink slacks. He watched for a few moments, then agreed. It was important that he win Calvin's confidence.

16

Carlyle drove, Gerri-Ann (his girl?), in a light blue coat with some kind of fur collar, beside him. Calvin sat in the death seat, his arm lying on the seat, his hand, one finger ringed, just behind Carlyle's wine-colored shoulder. Glora and Rochelle (who seemed to be Calvin's girl) flanked Mitchell in the back. He could feel Glora's soft hip through slacks and outer coat. Rochelle's legs were crossed, and something—perhaps the clasp of her garter belt—was digging into him. They were leaving Harlem.

"How you doing there?" He could see Calvin's face in profile, the darkness equalizing his color, his hooked nose making him a Jew.

Glora rested her red head on his shoulder. "He doing fine. Ain't you?" Her fingers were making their way through the spaces between the buttons of his overcoat, through his suitcoat, to his shirt. Sharp nails caught in the bandagelike material of his undershirt.

"Yes." The street sign told him he was on Eighth Avenue. Then the neon signs ended and he saw the low stone wall of the park, behind it trees.

The back seat was shrinking. Rochelle seemed constantly to cross, uncross her legs. He glanced at her, found her staring at him, nodding her head. She uncrossed, recrossed her legs again, then suddenly turned away; he was looking at the back of her head, the hair in the kitchen cut into a V.

He sank down into the seat, enjoying Glora's hand massaging his stomach. So this was how Black people were by themselves. He had often seen carloads of them, had wondered where they were going, what they would do when they got there. Now he was finding out.

Then Carlyle had stopped, was parking the car. They climbed out onto the pavement, cold even through his shoes. Mitchell was still wedged between the two girls.

He dozed in the elevator, the three bourbons and two more besides, pressing his eyes shut. They woke him, made him walk—down the marble-floored hall, into Calvin's apartment, dropped him onto a large white leather sofa, put a drink into his hand.

He opened his eyes, the glass half-empty now, and watched Glora dance with Carlyle—too close, and he wondered if she was really

WILLIAM MELVIN KELLEY

his girl. He struggled to his feet, pushed Carlyle away, glimpsed her lavender lips before she rested her head on his chest; his hands slipped between the waistband of her pink slacks, his fingers pinched the elastic on her underpants.

The music stopped; he opened his eyes. Carlyle and Gerri-Ann were gone. So was Rochelle. Calvin sat in the middle of the sofa, rather small, looking uncomfortable. But he raised his glass to Mitchell, then pointed past him, nodding. Mitchell danced Glora in a circle until he could look down a hallway, where he knew he would find Calvin's guest rooms. He completed the circle, to signal Calvin he understood, but Calvin had disappeared.

Of course, Glora wanted to make love to him, had been flirting with him all evening, but he was not quite sure how to introduce the topic. With Tam, he had waited politely until she showed him that she would not reject him. She had been working as a reader in a publishing house then, had invited him to her apartment for dinner. They had finished a bottle of good wine, listened to some Brahms, talked, necked. Then she had guided his hand to her breast.

But this was a Black woman. He tried to remember what the Southerners he had known in the Service had told him about Black women. But even their experiences had been somewhat different. Glora was not a prostitute, and he was not planning to rape her.

The answer was simple enough—so simple in fact that he realized he must be quite drunk not to have found it immediately. Glora thought he was Black. He would simply do and say what he thought Carlyle, Calvin, or perhaps even Cooley, would do and say in the same circumstances. There was even some justice in it. Cooley had taken advantage of Tam's unhappiness. Now he, Mitchell, would take advan-tage of one of their women. He would convince Glora to help him find Cooley.

He began by sitting her on the sofa, his arm around her. "You never told me where you work."

"Huh?" She had been leaning, snuggling against him. She sat up slowly, blinking.

He smiled, tried to relax his face. "I asked you where you work?"

"Why you want to know that?" Before he could answer, she asked him for a cigaret. He gave her one, held a light for her, staring at her over the flame.

"I want to know as much as I can about you."

She took a drag, her lips leaving lavender on the white filter. "Why?"

He shrugged. "I think I'll be moving to New York soon and I want to see you again."

She gave him her golden smile. "Your wife won't like that a bit." Before he could ask how she knew he was married, she answered him: "Carlyle told me. He say you got a little boy." She leaned toward him, put her arms around his neck, smeared lipstick from one side of his mouth to the other. "But what I care! Maybe you'll give me a baby too, and have to come visit me."

His plan seemed to be working. He put his hand under her sweater, whispered. "Why don't"—clearing his throat—"why don't we find an empty room."

She stood up, took his hand and pulled him to his feet, smiling, and led him down the hallway, past several closed doors, where he guessed he would find Carlyle, Calvin, and their girls. They entered the last room. She closed the door, walked to a low dresser, and looked at herself in the mirror.

Then she placed her fingers to her temples, as if to hold a headache, and lifted away her red hair. Underneath, her hair was black, kinky, a round lamb hat.

For some reason, it frightened him, and he took a step backward, trying to recover himself. "I wouldn't have guessed that."

She was proud. "I know. It's a good one. I saved for six months." She crossed her arms over her breasts, grabbed the bottom of the yellow sweater. Her head popped from the neckband. Her bra, against copper skin, was light green.

Lurking near the door, he watched her go to the bed, fold back the spread. The light green straps blinked like neon. When she had finished preparing the bed, she sat down, looked at him. "Anything wrong?"

He was trying to think of what Cooley would say, but the Cooley of his imagination remained silent. "I want to tell you about my wife." He wished immediately that he had not said that.

"Now?" She reached for the button on her pink slacks.

"Only that she's a bitch." He enjoyed saying it, even if it was a lie.

"I know that." She stood up, slid the slacks down over her thighs. "If she wasn't, you wouldn't be here, right?"

"Why, yes." Her underpants were lemon yellow. He closed his eyes. Opening them, he found her no more than a foot away, her arms spread to him. "I'll make up for that."

He backed up, but she kept coming. "Wait." She put her hands on his waist, began to pull his shirt out of his pants. "Do you know Cooley?"

She stopped, his shirttail between her fingers. "Cooley? Why . . . yeah, I know him." She looked confused, retreated to the bed, and sat down. Cooley certainly had a profound effect on people.

Sensing that he had thrown her off guard, he followed her. "Do you know where I can find him?"

"Look, honey, I don't want to get myself in no mess."

He sat down beside her, put his arm around her, speaking softly. "There won't be any mess. I just want to talk to him."

"About what?"

Perhaps he could tell her the truth, not that he was white, which, after the way he had completely deceived her would be too much for her, but everything else. Of course, he did not trust her. But after all she was sitting beside him almost naked, obviously had some feeling for him. He searched her face, realizing suddenly that he had seen it before, many times. The Black girl who worked in the file room at his office had the same face, and all of the girls he saw on the subway. They were all stupid, simple girls. Each wanted only a good job, a nice home, some bright clothes. And they were willing to do almost anything to get them. He need only give her a glimpse into his world and she would tell him everything he wanted to know. "I asked you before, where do you work?"

She bit her lip. "I ain't got a job."

"How would you like a nice job in a good company?" He was stroking her plump, soft arm.

"I couldn't get no job like that." Already her dark eyes could see herself riding the subway downtown.

"Yes, you could, with my help." He kissed her ear; she tried to move away, but he held her. "I want to tell you a secret, Glora. Originally,

I'm from Canada, but now I live in New York." She did not seem surprised. "And I work in a big company downtown." He remembered a movie he had seen a long time before. "I'm passing for white."

"Really?" She smiled.

"Now, I'll get you a good job in my company and all you have to do is tell me where I can find Cooley."

He saw fear in her eyes now. "Why you want to find him?"

"If I tell you, you have to promise not to tell anyone, except Cooley. You do want that good job, don't you?"

She nodded.

He sighed, hating to mouth the words, especially to someone like this. "My wife just had his baby."

"She really is a bitch, ain't she?"

He did not reply, knowing she would never understand all that had happened between him and Tam. "And I want Cooley to take the baby."

"Bye-bye job." She shook her head. "Cooley won't want no baby."

"I think he'll want this one." He decided not to tell her why. Then she would know he was not Black. Cooley might not want just any woman's baby, but this was Tam's baby — half-white. Of course he would want the baby. "It's a good job." And it would be nice to have her indebted to him, close at hand. "Well, what d'you say?"

"What you think, honey?" She tossed herself into his arms, pushed him down onto the bed, began to kiss his face. "And I'll be good to you too." She was on top of him. He inhaled her perfume, smiling, and reaching around her back, unhooked her bra. She began to undress him.

Both naked, they slid under the covers. He could not take his hands out of her hair; it pushed against his fingers like sponge. At first he found it distasteful, but then began to enjoy it. Between kisses, she kept talking. "So you ain't from Canada. You had me fooled. I bet you really fool those white folks downtown. You so cool. And you wait until I get there. All you got to do is call me in your office. 'Glora, will you bring me them letters from so-and-so company?' I'll have my pants down before you can close the door. One time, I was working downtown, in a mail-order house, for a little white man. He looking at me all the time. So I figured maybe it'd be good for a raise and I ran into him one night, accidentally." She winked down at him. "He took me up to his place and made his play for me. You thank God you never had to make it with no pasty-faced white man." She laughed so hard she rolled off him, and almost off the bed. She crawled back to him, rested her spongy head on his chest. "Let me tell you, honey, going over, he squeal like a little fat pig: eeee eeee eeee!" She started to laugh again. "That was the last time. I bet if any white man even get close to me, I'd know it. Eeee eeee eeee! You sure you ain't passing for colored, Mitchell?"

He denied it, trying to joke, but felt as if she had thrown ice water on his stomach and thighs. For the next fifteen minutes, he tried to recover. It was hopeless. Finally, he sat up.

She looked at him from the pillow, bewildered, perhaps a little angry.

He knew that unless he gave her a reason, she would not help him, might even turn against him. "It's an old war wound," he explained. "I never know when it's going to hit me."

She sat up, her face softer, and hugged him. "Sure is terrible the sacrifices a man got to make for his country." She kissed his shoulder. "You call me when you get over it."

He dressed, took her phone number, kissed her good-bye, all the while trying to avoid her dark eyes. "I'll be all right. I'll call you tomorrow, about Cooley."

"You do that, honey." She smiled, but suddenly buried her face in the pillow. Her back began to shake, short quick little shakes as if she was giggling. He had really disappointed her.

Outside, the sky was gray, the trees in the park black. He found his car and drove home, surprised to discover that the distance between Calvin's house and his own was less than a mile.

17

The door to his apartment was open. In his mind, Mitchell saw the Black thief going through their things, emptying drawers onto the floor, his heavy shoes walking on Tam's slips and bras. When she came home from the hospital and learned what had happened, she would never forgive him.

He wondered if the thief was still in the apartment. In an umbrella stand just inside the door, he found a heavy cane he had used after he injured his leg. He armed himself, crept deeper into the apartment. Behind the bedroom door, he heard voices.

Perhaps he should phone the doorman for help. But the doorman would disapprove if Mitchell did not handle the situation alone. In a day, the entire building would know he was a coward. Besides, they were robbing his apartment. He had to protect his own property, could expect no help.

He got a good grip on the cane, and opened the door.

The women lounged on the bed, larger now than he remembered it. Tam's mother was sitting, freckles and nipples above the covers, two pillows behind her head, her arm around the shoulder of a white woman with a simple blond pageboy. ". . . how easy it was for us." She kissed the top of the blond's head. "You haven't got a thing to worry about. He can be very sweet. Besides, you're married. All you have to do is let him guide you through it. He knows all there is to know about it."

"Do any buddy wants some twin to ache?" Opal was outside the covers, near the foot of the bed. She lay on her stomach, hatching her two large, brown breasts with her body.

"Hurricane you think of voodoo now?" Glora's head, red but kinky, was on his mother-in-law's shoulder.

"She's right, you know." Tam's mother turned away from the blond for a moment. "You ate too much rice."

"I kent hep

it if I, honey." She put her face into her folded arms.

Glora crawled to the foot of the bed, began to stroke Opal's back. "She frying."

The blond stared at them for a moment. "But we don't do things like this up state."

"We didn't do them when I was a girl either." Tam's mother smiled. "But you don't have to worry. Would I make you do something that was against the law?"

"Mitchell hair." Glora looked up from Opal's back. Opal peeked at him over her arm.

The blond seemed concerned. "He's not going to stop it, is he?"

"Mitchell?" Tam's mother made a face. "Don't be silly. Come here and give Mother a kiss."

He approached the bed, bent down, tried to escape with kissing her cheek. But she turned her head, caught his puckered lips between her teeth.

Finally she allowed him to stand up. "I'd like to speak to Tam, if I could." He realized his lip was cut.

"She's busy, dear. Why don't you come back in an hour or so."

"An hour!" The blond was angry. "I thought you said she'd be out in twenty minutes. Every time I come to New York I get cheated."

"You listen to me, young woman. You're a guest in my daughter's home. We're trying to be kind to you." Her breasts were much nicer even than Tam's. "But don't take advantage of us. I haven't even gone yet myself." The skin was stretched tight across her cheeks.

"Where's Tam?" Mitchell turned to Glora, found her looking at him, smiling faintly.

"She won't tell you anything, Mitchell. Not after the way you've treated her."

"But I didn't hurt her. I could've beaten her." He looked at Glora, who had begun to massage Opal's back. Under

Glora's fingers, the brown skin slid a few inches, then freed, snapped back into place.

"When did you come home from the hospital, Mitchell?" Tam was standing behind him, her arm around Cooley's waist, his hand on her shoulder.

"Can I talk to you for a minute, Tam?" He took a step toward her. But she had turned her back, was standing on tiptoes to kiss Cooley good-bye and thank him. He lifted her off the floor, over his head, kissed her stomach, and set her down.

"Is it my turn now?" The blond was sitting up, her feet on the floor.

Sadly, Mitchell began to remove his clothes. He did not really want to get involved in all this, but there were three white women, two Black women, and only Cooley. He had to do his part.

Opal sat up, watched him for a minute, then turned to Cooley and began to scream. "Why you slumming around baking tremble?"

Cooley left Tam, and knelt beside the bed, his head bowed. Opal stroked his hair. There was something sticky on her hand and his hair came out like the fur of dead dandelions.

The blond was standing over Cooley, hitting his shoulder with a shoe. "Come on, you can't get out of it."

He looked up, fear pinching the corners of his tiny eyes, then kissed Opal and stood up. He grabbed the blond's arm, white flesh oozing between his fingers, and dragged her from the room. Mitchell listened, heard nothing. He was undressed now, but could find no hangers for his clothes and asked Tam if she had seen any.

"Give them here, for God's sake." She took his clothes in a bundle and walked to the closet. She had no buttocks; they had been flattened by her girdle. There was no curve between the small of her back and her knees. She hung up his clothes, taking care that the fronts of his overcoat, jacket, vest, shirt all faced in the same direction.

Mitchell watched her bending to place his shoes side

WILLIAM MELVIN KELLEY

by side, heels together, on the closet floor. Deciding that he might as well start with her, he joined her at the closet, dropping his hand lightly on her back.

"No thank you, Mitchell. I've just finished." She closed the closet door. "Mother, do you want Mitchell?"

"Why of course, dear." Tam's mother smiled, opened her arms to him. The closer he got to her, the older she looked. She seemed to shrink, her back to hunch, her breasts to fall. Her freckles grew, becoming splotches of mold.

Glora had left Opal, was racing Mitchell to the head of the bed, a hairbrush in her hand. "Can't be burrowed with her head."

Mitchell watched Glora, her breasts hanging like water-heavy brown paper sacks. He tried to stop her before she reached Tam's mother.

But she shook her head. "Canned at this mint."

"This has got to stop now." The freckles on his mother-in-law's chest looked like tiny scars. "I'm very proud of you, Mitchell. We'll do something about you in a moment." She began to cry. "Doesn't anyone want my son?"

Opal sat cross-legged at the foot of the bed, her hands on her knees. "Suretainly." She stretched out on the bed, spread-eagled, an operation scar coiling across her stomach, disappearing into her navel.

"Well, Mitchell, go on. See what you can do." Tam shoved him and he fell on top of Opal, struggled to the surface, caught his breath. Opal put her arms around him, began to rock him, humming. Her breasts rose on either side of his head.

The women watched his every move.

"I'm glad I didn't get myself too deeply involved, Mother." Tam was shaking her head. "Look at that, will you?"

"Be patient, dear, he's just started." But she did not seem to believe that he would actually get better.

Glora was whispering into Opal's ear. "It won't take. So long, Old pal."

Opal turned her head, seemed quite ill. "But I fill so wick."

Glora stroked her shoulder. "Yule get wealthoon." Then to Mitchell. "Whorey up and fish pastry."

Mitchell was trying to bring Opal to life. But she lay under him, warm as new bread, bone lost in fat, and she would not move.

"Oh, that's terrible. Is that how we look, Mother?" Tam lay beside them, her head on her arm. "Terrible, Mitchell." She tapped his shoulder. "You should really study harder. I bet if I asked him, Cooley would show you what you're doing wrong."

He tried to be polite, and answer her, to tell her that he did his best, but he was becoming very excited and wanted to finish. He tried to move a little faster.

The women were gathered around Opal's head, wiping her face, trying to close the cuts over her eyes with petroleum jelly, giving her water from a soda bottle. "Just hold on, Opal. You can last."

Then the phone, the phone, the phone . . .

"Answer the phone, Mitchell." Tam grabbed him around the waist, tried to pull him out of Opal. "The phone."

"Just a minute. I'm almost finished." He tried to push her away. "God damn it, Mitchell, answer that phone!"

Opal came to life, placed her hands on his shoulders, pushing. "And saw the foam, Mr. Purse."

"Just let me finish, please." Opal shook her head, closed her legs under him. Tam shook her head. Glora shook her head. Tam's mother shook her head. "You have responsibilities, Mitchell."

He reached for the phone.

WILLIAM MELVIN KELLEY

18

As if to continue his dream, he pulled the receiver under the covers. "Hello." He did not want to open his eyes. Perhaps he had not yet lost Opal.

"Mitchell? Wake up, Mitchell." It was Tam's mother. "Wake up now."

"Oh, hi." He could still see her clearly, the two of them, Tam's mother and Opal. "How are you?"

"Are you awake, Mitchell?" She sounded stern. "I have something to talk over with you." He wondered if she was phoning from her bed in Washington. It was a beautiful bed, of dark wood, the headboard carved.

It seemed almost impossible that she expected him to have found Cooley, made an arrangement with him, in less than two days. "I've been trying, Mother. But you understand, don't you? I mean, it might take a little time."

"Keep quiet, Mitchell. I'm not calling about that." She stopped, but he did not speak; she would continue. "I'm with Tam."

He opened his eyes, pushed the sheet and blanket away from his face. "In New York? I thought you went back to—"

"I did. But Tam's doctor called a few hours after I got home. Where were you, Mitchell?" Her voice was flat, hard. "He said he tried to get you."

"I was in the Bronx, trying to find Cooley." His clothes were piled in an upholstered chair across the room. He had been too tired, too disappointed about Glora to hang them up. "We decided I was supposed to find him." He paused. "Didn't we?"

She sighed, a roar on the wire. "Yes, Mitchell. You are awake now, aren't you?"

"Yes, Mother."

He heard her suck in, pulling air from his end of the line. "One of the children died at six yesterday, Mitchell."

"Died?" That was all he could say for a moment. Then he realized that he was not saddened by the news. He wondered which of the babies had died, and after a respectful silence, asked her.

"Yours."

"Oh." He lay in bed, on his stomach, wondering why he still did not feel sad. Perhaps it was simply that he did not really know the baby, had seen it only once, had never held it. He wondered how he would feel if Jake died.

"You do understand what I've told you, don't you?"

He did not answer, and studying her voice, was quite surprised to discover her words were being filtered through some small amount of sadness.

He rolled from his stomach to his side. "How, Mother?"

"I don't really know. Some lung defect. The doctor said he couldn't have found it unless he was looking for it. It just died."

"I understand." Still, this was all he could say. None of the customary condolences applied, especially since normally he should be receiving them. "I'm sorry, Mother." He realized then he had forgotten about Tam. He asked how she was taking it.

"Very well. She hasn't shed a tear. She's being very brave."

"Should I come over?"

"That's not necessary. As a matter of fact, it would probably do more harm than good. She's calm now and visitors might just upset her."

He wanted to see Tam, but decided not to insist. He had already done her enough harm. "So it just happened, is that it?"

"Yes. That's what I said, isn't it?"

"Well," he hesitated for a second, "how's the other one?"

"Oh, fine. You say you haven't found this Negro yet?"

"No, Mother. Really. But I will soon." For an instant, he could see Glora's light-green bra standing out against her copper skin.

"All right." She took another deep breath. "You come by tomorrow. That will be better. Everything's under control here. Good-bye, Mitchell." She hung up.

He cradled the receiver, looked at the ceiling. Tam was really quite a remarkable woman. Both of them were, but especially Tam. Not only had she endured all he had done to her, but now the baby's death. He had a lot to make up. The next morning he would start; he would find the nicest cemetery plot in the city, would choose the best small white coffin. Today, he would find Cooley and get him to take the baby. Then he and Tam could start as close to fresh as possible. The last two years had been a mistake, and somehow it had all started with his firing Opal. But tomorrow Opal would come to work.

He climbed out of bed and began to dress, still wondering why he was not more moved by his baby's death. He knew feelings were hidden inside him, feelings he was too cowardly to recognize or face.

Dressed now, he went to the kitchen and began to make himself some breakfast. He opened the door to the refrigerator, searched the shelves for some eggs. He would see that the baby's coffin was lined with the best white satin.

The eggs were in a carton on the top shelf, near a roast, gray now with cold. He took two eggs to the table next to the stove, cracked the first into a bowl. The shell of the second seemed tough. Red-tinged egg white had already dropped into the bowl, before he noticed the embryo. He could see one eye, too big for its transparent body. He flushed both eggs down the toilet, and wandered into the living room.

Not only had he caused Tam pain by all he had done, but he had given her a defective child. As long as Cooley's baby was in their possession, she could never forget or forgive him. Someday, if he worked hard enough, the memory of those two babies and what they stood for in their lives might blend with the rest of the past. But now he knew they could never really start again, new. There was always some damage after an explosion.

When he had finished crying, he went to the phone and dialed Glora's number. "Glora, this is Mitchell Pierce."

Silence on the other end, a hand over her receiver, then: "Hello, honey. How you doing?"

"Fine." He did not have much time now. "Have you reached Cooley?"

Again, a silence. "No, honey. But Calvin have. He's here now. You want to talk to him?"

Calvin had probably driven her home. "Sure."

"Hello, man, how you been?"

"All right. How are you?" He did not wait for an answer. "You've been in touch with Cooley?"

"I just left him. He don't want to see you."

"Why not?"

"Look, man, he knows why you want to see him." Glora had betrayed him. And Calvin must have realized that Mitchell would be smart enough to figure that out. "Now, don't get mad, Mr. Pierce. She had to tell him. She thought she was helping you. We all trying to help you. But I bet you think we trying to get some money or something out of you."

"No, no." Perhaps he was being too suspicious.

"Anyway, we told him and he don't want to see you."

He had to see Cooley. His entire future depended on it. "Did you tell him there might be some money in it? I told Glora that."

"Yeah, I told him, but . . . look, why don't you just forget it. I'll tell you the truth. I don't think it'll work out for you. Cooley don't want no baby."

"But if I can just talk to him." He was pleading, but did not care.

Calvin hesitated. "Look, I can't promise you a thing. But maybe I can get him to come by your place. That way if he don't want to see you after that, you won't know where he is. But I tell you, he probably won't go for it."

Mitchell was tired of the whole business. It could drag on for months, and the longer Tam had the baby, the harder it would be to convince her to give it away. "Well, try anyway."

"Sure, man. We'll do everything we can."

"Let me give you my address."

Calvin laughed. "I don't mean no offense, Mr. Pierce, but Cooley'll know where you live."

19

Less than an hour later, the doorman called up from the street to tell Mitchell that a Negro, as he called him, wanted to see him. Mitchell was surprised; Calvin had been so certain that Cooley would not want to see him. He told the doorman to send the Negro up.

He stood by the door, listening for the elevator, wondering how different Cooley would look from his memory of him. There would be some small degree of distortion, and besides, a year and a half had passed. Mitchell was always startled, when looking at the pictures of his wedding, how much he had changed in five years, the gradual thickening of his features, his back slightly more stooped.

Finally the elevator arrived, but he could hear no footsteps on the hall carpet. He waited until the chimes rang, then opened the door.

Calvin was shaking his head. "No good, man. He didn't go for it."

For a few seconds, long after he had compared the face in his mind to the face before him, Mitchell could still see Cooley. Calvin was much shorter than he remembered Cooley, and much thinner, but even then, for a second or two longer, he saw Cooley. He cleared his mind, accepted disappointment, and asked Calvin in.

"Not a bit of it, man. He laughed at me. 'Let the white bastard rot!' he kept saying, and laughing." Calvin walked by him, his head bowed, his face thoughtful. "I tried, man. I really did." Mitchell followed him into the living room, watched him sit down in the antique chair.

"Excuse me, Calvin, but would you move to the sofa? That chair's liable to fall apart. My wife doesn't like anyone sitting on it." He shook his head, smiled. He did not want to hurt Calvin's feelings. "I don't know why we keep the damn thing anyway."

"Sure, man, I understand." Calvin was already crossing the room. "I was married myself one time."

Mitchell sat across from him, in a chair, patted himself for a cigaret, offered one to Calvin (who did not smoke), and leaned forward, elbows on his knees. "Is that all he said?" He did not really want to know, not today. Knowing that he had given Tam a defective baby was enough. But he knew now that finding Cooley would take at least a few weeks;

and whatever Mitchell knew about him would help.

Calvin shrugged. "No. I spoke to him for a couple minutes, but that's what it came to."

"What else did he say?"

Calvin stared at him for a long moment. His eyes seemed warm, his face calm. Suddenly, Mitchell realized that Calvin did not want to say anything that might hurt him. He really must have tried to convince Cooley to come to Mitchell's house. Remarkable, that once a man had overcome the fear and suspicion of these people, they could be quite loyal.

"Go on, it doesn't matter. I mean, it can't get any worse."

Calvin nodded. "Yeah, I guess so." He smiled, began to laugh, cut himself off. "This is real funny. I been a race man all my life. I mean, I do my share of getting the white man." He looked at Mitchell again, shaking his head. "But this time, honest to God, I'm for you, man. I mean, I couldn't tell you where to find him. Cooley and me live in the same world, and, well, you know . . . honor among thieves and all that. But you got to see that if I set Cooley up for you, I'm a dead man. No one could protect me. But if you find him on your own, I'd be happy for you. I bet I even know why you want to give Cooley that baby. You trying to get your marriage together, right?"

Mitchell realized that it would be ridiculous to hide it. "Yes."

"Well, I'll give you the square business truth, you'll have to do it without Cooley helping you."

"Maybe so." But he did not believe it. Eventually, he would find Cooley. "Tell me what he said, Calvin."

"Okay, Mr. Pierce, if that's the way you want it." He shook his head. "Right from the beginning. I guess I got to his place maybe a half-hour ago. He was still in bed. You know he reads the finance section. I mean, he really know what's going on in this world. So, anyway, I break it down to him. You just want to see him, I say. He starts laughing, bouncing around in the bed with the papers rattling on his lap. He tells me to let you rot. So, like I say, I'm for you, and I was getting a little mad too. It's his baby, I say to him. Don't he got no feeling for it? He say, he wasn't making it with your wife for no baby. He got babies, a couple of them, by a couple girls, and he ain't married yet. But when he meets a woman he likes a whole lot, he gives her a baby and sends her money.

Your wife? He saw her and wanted to find out how someone that evil and messed up in the head would be in bed. It was so bad, and weak, he had to go back a couple times to make sure it was really bad as he thought it was the first time." Calvin stopped. "I'm sorry, man. This got to be some tough stuff to take."

"No, no." Mitchell wondered how Cooley could be so ungrateful.

"Okay. Well, I didn't give up. I tell him it's still his baby, no matter how he feel about the mother. I know for a fact he don't like all the girls who got his babies. You know, Glora got one of his babies, a little girl." So that was why she had been so upset when Mitchell mentioned Cooley. "Anyway, he says at least he liked them all at one time or another. But he never loved that Tam. At first, it was to see how it would be, then later, there was a few bucks involved. You know, like when he wanted to take a cab somewhere and needed a few extra dollars." Mitchell tried to keep his face calm; he would not show this man how he felt. "I mean, I know Cooley, and every so often he do get carried away with his story."

Mitchell nodded.

"But that still don't make it not his baby, I tell him. And for a minute, I think I got him. He stops laughing. Yeah, he guesses that's true. But he's got old scores to settle."

"Old scores?"

"Yeah. So I ask him, what do he mean? Did Tam or you do something to him?" Calvin shook his head. "Nothing like that. Old scores from four hundred years ago, for his great-granddaddy and his granddaddy. That's another thing about Cooley. He a long grudge-holding Black man. He don't never forget a slight. Like what old scores? Like having a wife or a girl you really love and then she gets big with a baby, and you happy as a champ. But when the baby comes, God damn, it ain't yours. You can't blame your woman; she a slave too. And you can't do nothing about it yourself. So you just eat shit, and you and your woman take and raise that kid. Then one day, after you and the baby get good and attached, its natural father up and sells it away from you. So you lost a kid, but you never really had one. So, he says, it's your turn."

"My turn? But why me?" Just then, for no reason that he could ever after understand, he saw the fat Black woman sitting beside the highway, shaking her head.

Calvin snorted, smiled. "That's funny, because he said you'd ask that. And he told me that when you did, I was to ask you why his great-granddaddy?"

"Well, I didn't do it." Mitchell was bewildered. "What do I have to do with all that?"

Calvin shrugged. "That's what I said. But he didn't go for it. He said that I could figure that out for myself. So here I am, empty-handed."

They did not speak for a moment. Mitchell tried to accept the idea that all this was happening to him because of things that had taken place four hundred years before. Then he realized that Calvin had not mentioned how Cooley had reacted to the offer of money, and asked about it.

"Yeah, I told him that. But he said he'd want some money just to come and see you. In advance. I laughed at him. I mean, that was just too much. I told him you'd never go for that."

But Mitchell was excited. "No, wait a minute." He still believed that if he could see Cooley, could talk to him, he could convince him to take the baby. And somehow he sensed that Cooley knew this too. That would explain why Cooley dared not even see him. "How much would he want just to come see me?"

"Cooley? I bet I could get him down here for fifty dollars. I could put it to him this way: You'll give me some money if I arrange a meet, and there's fifty dollars in it for him. He might do it for me."

"Then we'll try it." Mitchell excused himself and went into the bedroom. In the closet, in one of Tam's hatboxes, he found their strong box. He always tried to keep at least one hundred dollars in tens in the box, for use in an emergency. He counted out seventy dollars and returned to the living room. "Now, here's fifty dollars for Cooley. And twenty for you. So there is money in it if you arrange a meeting." He looked at Calvin for a moment. "And even if you don't."

Calvin stood up, taking only five of the bills. "I don't want your money, Mr. Pierce."

"No, no, take it." He jammed the money into Calvin's breast pocket.

Calvin nodded, took the two bills out of his pocket, folded the seven neatly and put them into his pants. "Listen, Mr. Pierce, I'll go right up and see him. You call me about ten tonight." He asked Mitchell for pencil and paper, and wrote down his number. "Maybe by ten I'll have some news for you." They were standing in the foyer.

"All right. And thanks." He wondered if he and Calvin would ever meet after all this was over. Probably not. It would remind him of Cooley.

"Then, I'll see you." Calvin pushed through the swinging door which led to the kitchen. Mitchell followed. They shook hands at the delivery entrance, and Mitchell heard Calvin going down the smooth, gray cement stairs. When the cellar door thundered shut, he stepped back into the apartment.

20

He had reached the bedroom before he began to wonder how Calvin had known exactly where to find the kitchen, and the delivery entrance, and why it had been so easy for him to unlock the door. All three locks stuck, had to be shaken in a particular way. When he and Tam moved in, Mitchell's touch had been inadequate for months. Then he realized that he had seen Calvin's phone number before, and not too long ago.

Suspicious, he went to the phone table and leafed through the small white pad, through pages of Tam's signature, until he found the one page on which, several times, she had written the name Tam Johnson. He compared the phone number on that page to the one Calvin had given him.

He sat down.

On Sundays he liked to watch the educational programs on television. Perhaps that was where he had learned that, being superstitious, Black people often named their children after the rich and famous, presidents, athletes, movie stars. Calvin Johnson had been named after the thirtieth President of the United States, Calvin Coolidge; Cooley was a nickname.

He picked up the phone and dialed Calvin's number. The recording came on almost immediately. "The number you have reached is not a working number. If you want any assistance . . ."

For a while, still at the phone table, he thought about calling the police and reporting that he had been robbed of seventy dollars. He could say that a Calvin Coolidge Johnson had forced his way into his home at gunpoint. But the police would want to know how he knew the name of the bandit, and without the name they might never find him. He knew he could not give an adequate description. The faces of Calvin Coolidge Johnson and his own imaginary Cooley were now hopelessly mixed. He would not be able to keep the whole story from the police. He might even have to testify at a trial. He might lose his job.

He turned his back on the phone, went into the bedroom, and sat down in Tam's soft chair, trying to make plans. He would not fire Opal. Probably she knew nothing about this. But what Calvin Coolidge

Johnson knew, Carlyle would soon know. He would tell Opal. It was much better to have her working for him, dependent on him. In a few days, he would take Opal to the hospital, and she would carry the baby past the doorman, the people waiting for cabs in the lobby. They would say that Tam had given birth to one baby, and that it had died. The funeral would convince their friends of that. Then, they would say that eighteen months before, they had fired Opal because she had begun to date a Negro they did not like or trust. Opal had not learned her lesson until the Negro made her pregnant, and deserted her. She had come to them begging for help. They had taken pity, rehired her, consented to let her keep her illegitimate child in their house.

After he had worked it out, reviewed it a second time, he phoned down to the doorman and asked him if he would be so kind as to have someone bring up the bassinet in their storage locker.

The doorman was delighted. "So, they'll be coming home soon, huh? You must be real proud, Mr. Pierce."

For an instant, Mitchell did not know if he could do it—not without his voice snagging on something in his mouth. He found his hand pulling the receiver away from his head, found himself eyeing the cradle. But then he was pressing the slightly warm black plastic to his ear. "It isn't for Mrs. Pierce. We lost our baby. To a rare lung disease." He listened to his own voice, grading its sincerity, grief, bravery.

"Oh, that's too bad, Mr. Pierce. God, I . . ."

Mitchell could not give him time to recover. "It's our new maid. Who needs the bassinet. She has a new baby."

"Is that so?" The doorman was interested. "That's very nice of you, Mr. Pierce."

"Nice of me?"

The doorman cleared his throat. "Why, sure. I mean, for you to take in a stranger's kid in your time of sorrow and all."

He could not overreact to the compliment. "Well, it was an arrangement we made before the . . ."

"Still, Mr. Pierce. It'll be pretty tough on the nerves with a growing boy and two babies in the house."

"Two babies?" Mitchell did not understand. "But I told you we lost our baby."

"Both of them, Mr. Pierce?"

Somehow the doorman knew the truth. Eventually, through a network of maids and maintenance men, the entire building would know. But then, he did not speak to anyone in the building, did not care what they knew. And soon, they would move to the suburbs.

But he still had to discover how the doorman had found out about the twins. "Both of them? What are you talking about?" He fought to keep shrillness out of his voice.

"That's what the hospital said, Mr. Pierce." The doorman was nervous. "I mean, the management always calls the hospital and asks about our mothers."

"Well, the hospital was mistaken." He hoped he did not sound too abrupt for a grieving man.

There was a long pause; behind the doorman, a car was honking its horn. "That's funny, Mr. Pierce. Hospitals don't usually make mistakes like that."

A few sentences more and Mitchell began to believe he had convinced the doorman, and relieved, hung up. But in the quiet of the empty apartment, he was no longer certain. He had to think about it, perhaps make up an alternate story. He went to the bathroom to run himself a hot bath. When the water was gurgling out of the drain under the faucets, he twisted it off, undressed, and tested the tub with his foot. He turned out the light and pulled down the shade. He sank down deep into the hot water, and, on his side, his eyes closed and his hands clamped between his thighs, he filled the darkness with fantasies.

dəm